THE SANIBEL SUNSET DETECTIVE GOES TO THE MOVIES

Also by Ron Base

Fiction

Matinee Idol
Foreign Object
Splendido
Magic Man
The Strange
The Sanibel Sunset Detective
The Sanibel Sunset Detective Returns
Another Sanibel Sunset Detective
The Two Sanibel Sunset Detectives
The Hound of the Sanibel Sunset Detective
The Confidence Man
The Four Wives of the Sanibel Sunset Detective
The Escarpment
The Sanibel Sunset Detective Goes to London
Heart of the Sanibel Sunset Detective
The Dame with the Sanibel Sunset Detective
The Mill Pond
I, The Sanibel Sunset Detective
Main Street, Milton
Bring Me the Head of the Sanibel Sunset Detective
The Hidden Quarry
The Devil and the Sanibel Sunset Detective
The Sanibel Sunset Detective Saves the World

Priscilla Tempest Mysteries
(with Prudence Emery)
Death at the Savoy
Scandal at the Savoy
Princess of the Savoy

THE SANIBEL
SUNSET
DETECTIVE
GOES TO THE
MOVIES
RON BASE

West-End
Books

Library and Archives Canada Cataloguing in Publication

Title: The Sanibel sunset detective goes to the movies / Ron Base.
Names: Base, Ron, author.
Identifiers: Canadiana 20210273933 | ISBN 9781990058028 (softcover)
Classification: LCC PS8553.A784 S28 2021 | DDC C813/.54—dc23

West-End Books
133 Mill St.
Milton, Ontario
L9T 1S1

Text design and electronic formatting: Ric Base
Cover design and coordination: Jennifer Smith
Sanibel map: Ann Kornuta

"All Right, Mr. DeMille, I'm ready for my closeup."

Norma Desmond, *Sunset Boulevard*

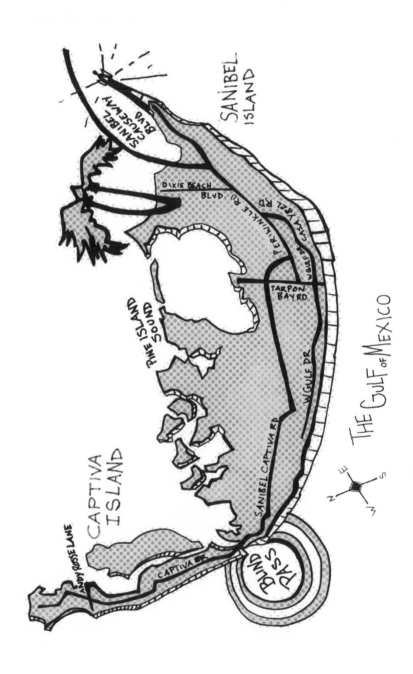

1

"Lower that bicycle seat a little more!" ordered an imposing heavyset man. He was bald, deeply tanned, wearing a pair of jodhpurs. He pushed past Tree Callister, marching briskly over to where a worker on a tall stepladder, set up beside a big wooden cross, was adjusting the seat mounted on the cross's upright beam.

"That better, Mr. DeMille?" the worker called down to the man in the jodhpurs.

"An improvement," DeMille announced. He turned as a tall, rake-thin man, bearded, wearing a wig like a helmet of elaborately styled brown hair, staggered into view clad only a loincloth. The bearded man straightened himself up somewhat when he saw DeMille. He worked to focus his bleary, red-rimmed eyes. "There you are, Cecil, old fellow. I am prepared. Are we set to go?"

As the balding man began to scowl, Tree recognized with a start that this was Cecil B. DeMille. The man swaying uncertainly in his loincloth was H.B. Warner, aka Jesus. The question was, Tree asked himself, what was he doing here? How had he ended up on the set of *The King of Kings*, DeMille's 1927 extravaganza about the life of Christ?

"Harry, you're drunk," DeMille declared accusatorily.

"Like hell I am," adamantly replied Warner in a disconcertingly plumby British accent. Not exactly the voice of Christ, Tree thought. Unless Christ, like Warner, attended Bedford School once he left the manger.

"Who the blazes do you think you are?" demanded DeMille.

"I am Jesus, the king of kings," Warner replied airily. His eyes rolled back and he started to collapse. Tree was close enough that he was able to catch Warner and hold him so that he didn't hit the floor. DeMille took quick note of Tree's intervention before turning to a hovering assistant. "Take Harry back to his dressing room, pour some coffee in him."

"Got you, Mr. DeMille."

The assistant lifted Warner out of Tree's arms. Warner began to come around. "What are you doing?" he demanded.

"We're taking you back to your dressing room, Harry," DeMille said angrily.

Two assistants began to drag him off. Warner resisted. "Unhand me, you cads," he yelled. "I am a star. You do not treat a star like this! I am Jesus Christ, for Christ's sake! Put me on the bloody cross, I demand the bloody cross!"

"Get him out of here!" DeMille boomed in a voice not to be challenged.

Warner promptly sagged against the two men supporting him. Together they hauled away the comatose actor.

DeMille lifted his eyes toward the heavens. "Forgive him Lord, he's a damned drunken fool." He then removed his eyes from the heavens and focused on Tree. "Thanks for helping out, friend. I imagine you must be the young Jesuit they said was coming over to watch the filming…"

"Well, I…" Tree started to say.

"It's fine," DeMille interrupted, his attention drawn to the cross on the far side of the soundstage. "Happy to have a pious young man of the cloth with us." He raised his voice to call to the crew member on the ladder who was adjusting the bicycle seat. "It's still too high, Mel." Mel adjusted the seat some more. Tree noticed that plaster hands had been attached to either side of the crossarm.

"We raise Harry sitting on that bicycle seat, that is if we can ever get him sober," DeMille explained to Tree. "Once he's up there, he slips his hands into those plaster hands already nailed to the cross, and we have Jesus where I need him."

DeMille shook his head. "I'm having to deal with a drunk Jesus, no money, a studio going down the drain, and everyone furious with me because of the way we're treating Mary Magdalene."

"As a beautiful courtesan?" Tree ventured.

DeMille gave him a surprised look. "You heard about that? Well, there you go." He stepped closer to Tree, eyes blazing. "They don't understand. Mary is *redeemed* in our telling of the story. Saved by the purity of Jesus. What do you think of that?"

Tree wasn't sure what to say. "That sure sounds like our Jesus," he finally sputtered.

DeMille seemed satisfied with the answer. "Let me tell you something, young man—and you can take this as gospel. This movie is the greatest story ever told. When it is finished, it will be like nothing you've ever seen before on the motion picture screen."

"I'm sure it will be," Tree said agreeably.

"This is the most significant topic of our time, and by God it will be the greatest movie of *all* time," DeMille went on, "This movie will *save* movies!"

As DeMille finished his speech, his assistant reappeared, looking extremely nervous. "What is it, Sal?" Demanded DeMille. "Where's Harry?"

"Mr. Warner is still passed out in his dressing room," Sal explained. "We haven't been able to wake him."

"That drunken fool," lamented DeMille. "He knows we've shot too much of him, I can't fire him so far into production. He's the Son of God, for Christ's sake, and this is how he treats the role of a lifetime?"

"He seems a little old," Tree ventured.

"What?" DeMille shot him a look. "What are you saying?"

"Jesus was a young man, wasn't he?" Tree was becoming as nervous as Sal the assistant. "Thirty-three years old, unless I'm mistaken."

"Harry doesn't look his age," DeMille mumbled. "I don't want to hear about age."

"Also, Mr. Warner is a white man," Tree put in.

DeMille's expression was one of horror this time. "What's that got to do with anything."

"You know, given the part of the world, Jesus would not have been white."

"We're all set to go, Mr. DeMille," Sal said, by way of saving DeMille from exploding.

Everyone around DeMille fell to silence. He bowed his fine head as if in prayer, then lifted his head setting fierce eyes on Tree. "You'll do," he pronounced. The word from, if not God, certainly Hollywood's most powerful filmmaker.

"Do what?" responded Tree in alarm.

"Despite your provocative questions, I must make use of you, young man."

"Make use of me?" Tree didn't like the sound of that.

"We need a long shot, and then we're done with the Calvary sequence." DeMille sounded as though he was thinking out loud. "No one will know."

"Know?" Tree asked. "Know what?"

"Undress this young man," DeMille ordered his underlings. "Get him a loincloth."

"But I can't do this," Tree stammered.

"You'll be just fine," DeMille affirmed. "All you have to do is sit on a bicycle seat and look sad because you're about to die for all mankind."

Before Tree could object further, Sal along with other crew members were on him, stripping off his clothing, simultaneously propelling him forward so that by the time he was pushed up the man-made slope supposedly representing Golgotha, he was naked. A middle-aged woman carrying a pale brown loincloth stepped forward, unimpressed with Tree's nakedness. "He doesn't look much like Harry," she opined giving him the fisheyed once-over.

"Never mind that now," said Sal. "Get the loincloth on him before the boss has a heart attack."

The woman proceeded to wrap the loincloth around Tree's naked torso. "That's a little better," she declared.

"Okay, up the ladder you go, pal," Sal said.

"I don't want to." Tree's spoke in a whiny voice. "I don't want to hang from the cross! I can't! I can't hang from the cross..."

"What?" asked a confused voice.

Tree opened his eyes. Freddie, his long-suffering wife, already dressed and looking radiant, hovered over him. "What's that about saving movies?"

"I was dreaming about Cecil B. DeMille," Tree said.

Freddie allowed a puzzled expression to mar what Tree, with some accuracy, considered the perfection of her face. "Who?"

"Cecil B. DeMille, the guy who practically invented movies."

"What about him?"

"He was trying to get me to wear a loincloth and hang from a cross so I could stand in for Jesus."

"Tree, what are you talking about? You are many things, however, a stand-in for Jesus, you are not."

"L.B. Warner was too drunk. DeMille put me on the cross. I was Christ being crucified," Tree said, sitting up, trying to clear his head.

"You and your dreams," Freddie said with an all-too-familiar roll of her eyes. "Come on, Tree up and at 'em. Today, your best friend starts to become famous. You don't want to miss that."

No, Tree thought as he lifted himself out of bed, he definitely did not want to miss that.

2

I'm *about* to be famous," announced Rex Baxter. "It's about damned time, too."

Rex made the announcement in the office he and Tree shared at the back of the Cattle Dock Bait Company at Punta Rassa, not far from Sanibel Island. Customers crowding the bait shack in the outer room were much more interested in acquiring bait for a day of fishing than they were in hiring a private detective or take much interest in a former Hollywood actor who was, finally, about to become immortalized on film.

That is, thought Tree, if anyone these days could be immortalized, given the rocky state of film.

The announcement of Rex's impending fame was occasioned by the arrival of a movie crew on Sanibel Island to begin filming a series for the Netflix streaming service based on Rex's memoir published a couple of years before.

In many ways, it could be argued that Rex was already famous. The former president of the Sanibel-Captiva Chamber of Commerce was a well-known figure on the two barrier islands along the west coast of Florida. He had been locally famous and much loved in Chicago for many years, first as the host of an afternoon movie show on the station and then as the TV weatherman who, he was the first to admit, didn't know much more about the weather than what he saw when he stuck his head out a window. But, as was often said, Rex's audience did not tune in for his weather reports. They tuned in for Rex.

"What was that?" asked Gladys Demchuk, making her daily late arrival for work as a combination office assistant and secretary, although, as Gladys liked to point out, no one called a secretary a secretary any more. Besides, when you're carrying a gun in your purse and you know how to use it, are you really a secretary?

"Rex is going to be even more famous than he is now," Tree said.

"Be careful what you wish for, Rex," Gladys offered, pushing her handbag under her desk. Rail thin, wearing her russet hair tied back, the former Blue Streak, was once a shining star of the adult film industry in Los Angeles. She had decided it was time to change her life, take back her own name and get out of town. She had ended up in Florida where she had been hired by Rex, supposedly to assist him with his book, and to answer the phone should anyone ever decide to call the Sanibel Sunset Detective Agency. Rex had shown more than a passing interest in a developing a relationship with Gladys, something that she had resisted.

"No, it's going to be fine," Rex maintained. "My life is being immortalized on film at the perfect time in my life."

"How's that?" asked Gladys.

"I'm too old to fall prey to the usual vices: drugs, alcohol, and women." He paused. "Hold on a minute. Let me amend that slightly. I'm still susceptible to women."

"Good to know," Gladys said coolly. "While you're making yourself susceptible to women, don't forget you're having lunch today at the Lighthouse with your producer, Clay Holbrook. Holbrook phoned me earlier this morning to say John Twist has arrived on the island. He's will be joining you."

"John Twist," said Rex with a frown. "The last of the living-breathing movie legends."

"I don't think there's much legendary about him," Gladys put in. "Unless you think a trouble-making drunk is worthy of legend status."

Rex gave her a sharp look. "You sound as though you know whereof you speak."

"Let's say it's something I'd as soon not talk about," Gladys said quietly.

"Still, he is coming out of retirement in order to play, let's say, the more... *mature* Rex," Tree offered. "The Rex looking back on his life and career as he lounges around Sanibel." Tree looked over at Rex. "I'd say that's quite a coup, getting Twist. He hasn't worked for years."

"I was in a movie with him back in the sixties," Rex said.

"You co-starred with John Twist?" Gladys asked, not entirely without sarcasm.

"I had one line: 'You're under arrest, pal.' I stole the movie."

"I'll bet you did," Gladys said, laughing.

"I don't know why I have to go along," Tree said. "This is your show, Rex."

"No, no," Rex said hurriedly. "I want you with me. Particularly if Twist is there."

"You don't like him?"

"Let's say I'm leery of him. I feel better having you along."

"Then I'll be there," Tree said.

Gladys busied herself carefully arranging three pens so that they were properly aligned on her desk. She did not look happy.

3

Whether John Twist was a legend—whether any man or woman who recites words written for them while standing in front of a camera could rightly be called legend—was open to debate, Tree reflected as he drove Rex to the Lighthouse Restaurant. Still, Twist was the last man standing among the screen stars of the late 1950s and 1960s.

In his movie-star heyday, Twist had a reputation as a notorious Hollywood wild man, big drinker, big life, lots of wives, lots of woman trouble. He hadn't made a movie for years, allbut forgotten until Rex's producers somehow convinced him—with lots of money, Tree suspected—to briefly return to work. He had come back to a much different movie world, the age of streaming that had changed everything. Twist was the dinosaur, brought briefly back to life.

"What do you suppose happened between Twist and Gladys?" Rex asked as Tree came into the Lighthouse parking lot.

"What makes you think anything happened?"

"I don't know," Rex said. "But the way she was acting back at the office when his name came up. Something happened."

"Whatever it was, if it was anything, it was a long time ago," Tree said, sliding the car into an empty space. "Gladys lived in another world back then."

"I guess I'm a little like Gladys," said Rex.

"What do you mean?"

"Nothing…I'm not looking forward to this lunch, that's all."

"Because of Twist?"

"It's nothing," Rex said hastily.

"What is it about Twist?" Tree pressed.

Rex waved a dismissive hand. "Let's get in there," he said. He opened the passenger-side door to get out, struggling a bit as he did. He wasn't moving with the same ease he did only a few months ago, Tree noticed.

Inside its broad, well-lit interior, the Lighthouse had already filled with lunching tourists. Tree waved to Matt, the bartender. Rex shook the hand of Roberto, one of the restaurant's longtime employees. They had been hanging around the place forever, Tree reflected. Or as forever as it got in Florida.

A hostess with a silky sheen of waist-length hair led them out to the terrace overlooking the marina. The producer, Clay Holbrook, already occupied a table. He stood as they approached, a slim, pale-faced man, black hair thinning and cut close to his scalp. Round-rimless glasses gave him a slightly academic air which Tree imagined didn't help him much in Hollywood. The industry was not exactly renowned as a bastion for academics. Holbrook broke into a delighted smile as he shook Rex's hand. "Great to see you again, Rex," he said enthusiastically. "Really excited about shooting on the island. Really excited."

The way he said it, Tree could almost believe him.

Rex accepted Holbrook's handshake without revealing a similar delight or excitement. He turned to Tree. "Meet my friend, Tree Callister. I thought he should come along today."

Holbrook responded by shaking Tree's hand with nearly the same enthusiasm he had brought to shaking Rex's. "Great to meet you, Tree. Can I call you, Tree? The famous Sanibel Sunset Detective. I've heard about you."

"You should make a movie about him," Rex suggested as he sat down.

"There you go," Holbrook said agreeably. "Not a bad idea.

Not a bad idea at all." He seated himself as he went on. "However, for now, let's get your story into the can, Rex. As they used to say in the bad old days when they actually put film in cans."

"Those were the days," Rex said.

"Yeah, I guess you've got firsthand knowledge of the way things were. You and Johnny. The two of you, what a combination. You're going to get along like a house on fire, I just know it."

"Where is Twist?" Tree asked.

"He'll be along," Holbrook said reassuringly. "You know, movie star time. Not the same as us mere mortals."

Holbrook leaned in, dropping his voice to a conspiratorial level. "Just a suggestion, of course, but how be we make this an alcohol-free lunch? That okay with the two of you?"

"I don't drink," Tree said.

"Fine with me," nodded Rex.

Holbrook sat back with a relieved grin. "I'm an ice tea guy myself. You know how it is."

"No, Clay," Tree said. "How is it?"

"Well, you know, we don't need to give Johnny any encouragement when it comes to, you know, alcohol."

"The way I hear it, he doesn't need encouragement," Rex said.

"Hey, I had a long talk with him before he signed on. Right now, he's on the wagon," Holbrook said smoothly. "This shoot is very important to him. He assures me he won't be drinking."

"Interesting," Rex said. He didn't sound convinced.

Inside the restaurant's main dining room, a sudden murmur of recognition rose. Moments later, John Twist, his white hair pushed back from a high forehead, swept onto the terrace. He marched forward with the trademark swagger that had thrilled audiences in the late 1950s and '60s, his shoulders thrown back, his large stomach held in as best as Twist could manage.

He was dressed in faded jeans and a flowing white shirt, untucked in a fruitless effort to hide his girth. Even at his advanced age, John Twist was every inch the movie star. A movie star, Tree reflected, from another era when male stars were men of authority and knew how to take command as soon as they arrived on the screen. Gregory Peck, Burt Lancaster, William Holden, Robert Mitchum, John Wayne, Charlton Heston, and John Twist all gave off assurances that they were in control. The audience could now relax, because no matter what happened, these men could overcome whatever hurdle was thrown in their way and make things right at the end of two hours. There was somethrooking oddly comforting about those guys, Tree thought, a comfort level that had been all but lost in contemporary leading men.

"Boys," he declared in a laconic drawl, as the others stood in greeting. Twist did not bother to shake hands but proceeded to occupy the empty chair at the table. "What's up?"

"Good to see you, Johnny," Holbrook said eagerly. He pointed at Rex. "Hey, I think you already know Rex Baxter."

Twist regarded Rex with what Tree could only describe as lazy insolence. Not particularly friendly, Tree thought.

"How are you, John?" Rex asked in a neutral tone of voice, neither friendly nor unfriendly.

"Why I'm doing just fine, Rex, never better," Twist replied distractedly, looking around. "Where does a fella get a drink around here?"

Holbrook looked abruptly nervous. He nodded at Tree. "Johnny, you haven't met Rex's friend, Tree Callister."

Twist eyed Tree lazily. "Tree? That your name."

"It is," said Tree.

"Never heard a name like that before." He allowed a vague smile. "How about it, Tree? Can you help me get a drink?"

As if on cue, Roberto appeared. He shook the hands of his two regulars without apparently recognizing Twist. "What can I get you gentlemen to drink?" he asked.

"Double Johnny Walker, no ice," Twist ordered promptly.

"Are you sure that's what you want, Johnny?" Holbrook asked anxiously.

"Oh, I'm sure, all right," Twist replied. "If I didn't want Johnny Walker, I wouldn't have ordered it, now would I?"

"It's just that you said—"

"I don't give a good goddamn what I said, I'm having a drink." The threatening growl in Twist's voice had struck fear in the bad guys he'd faced down in all those westerns he had made. If it didn't scare Holbrook, it succeeded in silencing him.

"I'll have San Pellegrino," he said quietly.

Tree and Rex ordered sparkling water. Roberto gave everyone a menu and went off.

"Rex was just telling us how excited he is that you've agreed to come out of retirement to play him," Holbrook reported, telling an out-and-out lie with an eagerness that was impressive if misguided, Tree thought.

Twist turned to Rex, regarding him with half-closed eyes. "Is that true, Rex? Are you excited?"

"Excitement doesn't begin to cover it," Rex said, deadpan, his eyes fixed on Twist.

Twist sat back with a laugh. "Bullshit," he said. Then he looked at Tree. "I still can't get over it."

"Over what?" Tree asked.

"Your name. A funny damned name, Tree."

"Tree is a private detective on Sanibel," Rex offered.

"Private detective? You don't say. They need private detectives around here?"

"Sometimes," Tree said.

"Tree, the private detective. Old Tree. Out there sleuthing. Getting a little long in the tooth for that sort of thing, aren't you, Old Tree."

"Some days I believe that's true," Tree replied, making sure to keep his voice level.

"I hear you," Twist said, breaking out a weary smile, "I hear you loud and clear."

"From what I understand from Rex, Tree is pretty well known around Sanibel for his various exploits," Holbrook said enthusiastically. He addressed Rex. "Tree works as your bodyguard, does he?"

"Yeah," Rex replied, deadpan. "I need all the protection I can get."

"Better be careful Old Tree," Twist said edgily. "Rex is gonna need protection from me."

"Is he?"

"Yeah," Twist replied without a hint of humor, "he is."

Rex stayed silent. Holbrook began to look more nervous.

Roberto arrived with the drinks. Twist polished off the Johnny Walker with a couple of gulps. "What's your name, son?" Twist demanded of Roberto.

"Roberto," he answered.

"Bring me another one of these, Roberto."

Roberto nodded and then asked, "Are you folks ready to order?"

Twist's face darkened. "Hey, you get me a drink, got it? Then you worry about the rest."

Tree could see Roberto's mouth tighten. Rex said, "It's

okay, Roberto. Please get Mr. Twist his drink and then you can take our orders."

Roberto offered something like a smile. "Coming right up," he said and turned away.

Roberto's hasty retreat reduced everyone to silence. Twist occupied himself examining his glass, as though in disbelief it was empty. Holbrook cast an apprehensive glance in Twist's direction. Tree, with nowhere else to look, eyed the menu he knew only too well. Holbrook finally exhaled and said, "Johnny, maybe you've got some questions for Rex, you know, anything that would help with filling out your character's background."

Twist responded by giving Rex one of his lazy glances that was either full of disdain or disinterest, Tree couldn't decide which. "Sure, I got some questions for Rex."

"Fire away," Rex said.

"You think I don't remember you." Twist's eyes glinted with malice.

"No reason why you should," Rex, as close to jumpy as Tree had seen him.

"You were the cop in that piece of shit crime thing I did back when dinosaurs roamed the earth and people still went to movie theatres."

"Depends on which piece of shit you're talking about," Rex acknowledged.

"The one you were in. And there was only one, right?"

"Yeah," Rex replied in a low voice.

"You had that one line, I remember," Twist said, nasty eyes on Rex. "Something about, 'I'm arresting you.' Wasn't that it?"

"'You're under arrest, pal.'" Rex's words escaped from between clenched teeth.

"Yeah, that was the line. Simple line. You kept blowing it."

"I never blew the line." Rex was practically whispering.
"Bullshit. You blew the line. You couldn't get it. We were on
the clock. Drove the director crazy. He was ready to kill you.'"
Rex said nothing. Tree saw that his friend's face had become ashen.

"Hey, memories from the past," Holbrook interjected with
what was becoming habitual nervousness where Twist was concerned. "Maybe it's time we all got some lunch into us." He
turned to motion for a server who was nowhere in sight.

Twist leaned forward, going in for the kill. "You were never
much of an actor, were you, Rex? Maybe that's why you never
amounted to anything. Maybe that's why you ended up a TV
weatherman in Chicago. Wait a minute." Twist leaned back,
eyes bright with anticipation. "You didn't know shit about
weather, either, did you?"

"Could be you're right, John." Rex spoke quietly. "But
here's where we are now. They're making a show about me, and
you're the one playing me. If you're a goddamn better actor
than me, here's your chance to prove it."

With that, Rex rose from the table, no sense of struggle this
time, moving with catlike ease as he strolled off the terrace into
the restaurant.

Roberto returned carrying Twist's drink. Sensing the tension at the table, he quickly placed the glass in front of the
actor and hurried away. Twist looked at the glass with satisfaction, picked it up and downed half its contents He smiled
blearily. "That bastard is right. If I'm going to be him, I'd better
be a better actor than he ever was." He shrugged. "I *am* a better
actor. I'm the movie star, and he never was."

"Yeah, but he's a great guy," Tree said, rising. "And you're
just an asshole."

He walked off the terrace.

4

That was an inauspicious beginning, Tree thought as he drove back to the office. The actor going out of his way to insult the person he was playing onscreen. An interesting but not very useful way to start a production. For all his talk about Hollywood and his stories of sleeping with Joan Crawford—the aging movie queen seducing the hot-looking young actor—Rex remained forever sensitive about his lack of success in Tinsel Town. You could tell great stories, but they didn't quite cover the disappointment of basically failing at your chosen profession.

He got out of his car close to a big white Hummer. Not often you saw one these days, he thought. But then if anyone was going to drive a Hummer it was bound to be someone in Florida.

He was considering what to say to Rex that would be consoling as he made his way through the Cattle Dock Bait Company, quiet at this time of day—the fisherman apparently were out fishing with the bait they had bought in the morning. But Rex wasn't in their office. Gladys was at her desk looking tense as she eyed the two men who sat close by. Tension at the Lighthouse, now more tension here as Tree raised a questioning eyebrow at Gladys.

"These gentlemen are here to see you," she said, and added unnecessarily: "They don't have an appointment."

"Sorry to barge in on you, Mr. Callister," said the older of the two men, rising from the chair. Pale and chubby, he wore a wide-brimmed white Stetson, beneath which his flushed face was rimmed with a carefully maintained salt-and-pepper beard. The man with him also stood. He was African-American, tall and skinny, his face defined in sharp edges—sharp cheekbones, sharp jawline. Those edges created deep hollows in his face and emphasized hooded, dangerous eyes. You might have a beer with the rotund salt-and-pepper-beard guy, Tree thought as he faced the two men. But you would almost certainly watch yourself around the skinny fellow with those dangerous eyes.

"I'm Shell Dean, Mr. Callister, and this gent with me, he's a valued associate of mine, Mr. Dix. That right, Mr. Dix?"

"You got that right," Mr. Dix said.

Shell Dean held out a meaty hand that took Tree's in a vise-like grip. Mr. Dix did not offer his hand. Those hooded eyes revealed nothing. They never left Tree.

"What can I do for you gentlemen?" Tree asked, moving away to give himself some distance—protection?—seating himself behind the safety of this desk.

"Do you mind if we take a seat?" Shell asked in his bright rumble of a voice.

"By all means," Tree said.

Shell sat across from Tree while Mr. Dix chose to remain in the background. Shell appeared to spend time making sure he was comfortable, straightening his jacket, adjusting the seam on his pantleg. "Now, why we are here today," he announced.

"That would be a good start," agreed Tree.

"As you can imagine when it comes to visiting a gentleman such as yourself, I've got a bit of a problem I'd like you to address." He shot a glance back at Dix. "That right, Mr. Dix?"

"We got a problem," agreed Mr. Dix.

"And what is that problem?" inquired Tree.

"The problem is my fiancée." Shell's voice lost much of its chipper tone. "Have I got that right Mr. Dix?"

"Fiancée, that's it," piped in Mr. Dix.

"April May," Shell expanded.

"April May?" inquired Tree. "That's her name?"

"It's the name she has adopted since coming to Nevada from her home in Georgia."

"Okay," Tree said.

"My fiancée April has disappeared. Is that about right, Mr. Dix?"

"You got it," asserted Dix.

"I'm sorry to hear that," Tree said.

"Disappeared *and* abducted," Mr. Dix interjected insistently.

"Yes, it's all very sad." Shell's tone had become mournful. "You might say my fiancée April is the light of my life. Is that about right, Mr. Dix?"

"Light of your life, correct."

"The fact that she has done this fills me with deep sadness and terrible angst."

"I can imagine," Tree said. "Where did she disappear? Here in Florida?"

"No, Nevada. I own several small casinos outside Reno. April was employed as a croupier at my Gold Dust Ranch Casino. Unfortunately, it was frequented by a good-for-nothing varmint who owns a ranch in the area. I believe he seduced my girl with his lavish lifestyle and then fed her drugs." That inspired another affirming glance in Dix's direction. "Got that right, Mr. Dix. Drugs?"

"Drugs." Dix, once again parroting his boss.

"I begged my April not to have anything to do with this varmint, but of course she wouldn't listen to good advice from the man who loves her."

"Damned good advice it was too," added Dix without prodding.

"What happened, Mr. Dean?"

"Tell you what happened." Shell leaned forward. His eyes were like burning coals. He glanced at Dix. "I'm gonna tell him, Mr. Dix."

"You tell him," Dix advised.

"The truth of what happened—April ran off with this son of a bitch, disappeared with him. That's goddamn well the truth of what happened."

"So this man didn't actually abduct your fiancée," Tree suggested.

"I wouldn't say that he abducted her… *exactly.*"

"No, that wouldn't be quite accurate." Dix again, unprovoked.

"Then what would you say?" asked Tree, puzzled.

"I would say that this no-good, son of a bitch has lured my April away to a life of sin and debauchery, a kind of abduction, if you will. I will not let this stand—"

"No, you will not," chimed in Dix.

"I have sworn to put a stop to this evil man, and bring my girl out of the darkness and into the light. Have I got that right, Mr. Dix?"

"Into the light," mimicked Dix.

"I see," Tree said slowly.

"I have been trying to locate this bastard for the past six weeks," Shell went on. "Now it turns out he is here in Southwest Florida."

"With your April?"

"As far as my associate here, Mr. Dix, and myself have been able to ascertain, that's affirmative. She is in the company of this devil."

"Here in the Fort Myers area, no question," threw in Dix.

"So, Mr. Dean," Tree said, focusing on his visitor in the

Stetson hat. "If you know the whereabouts of these women, why do you need me?"

Shell cast an impatience glance in Dix's direction. "Why do we need Mr. Callister, Mr. Dix? Tell him, please."

"Because although we know they are in Southwest Florida, in the Fort Myers area, Mr. Dean and I don't know *exactly* where they are located. That's where you come in." Dix aimed a bony pistol-like forefinger at Tree.

"You want me to find April?"

"That's entirely correct, sir." Shell had retaken command of the conversation. "I want you to find my April and return her to me."

"Once you do that, once you've found her, you will take no action," interjected Dix, "You will tell us where they are located and your job is done."

"What then?" Tree asked.

"Then Mr. Dean and I will take the necessary appropriate action." Dix spoke formally, as if from a script.

"What does appropriate action mean?'"

"That's something, sir, that is nothing you have to be concerned about," Shell said, taking over again. "Your job is merely to locate April."

"Okay, but do you have the identity of this man she is with?"

"What do you say, Mr. Dix, do we have a name?"

"We certainly do," replied Dix.

"Who is he?" Tree demanded.

"A no-good, bastard, son of a bitch named John Twist," declared Shell.

5

John Twist?" Tree was working hard to keep the words from choking in his throat.

"Apparently the son of a bitch used to be some kind of actor. That right, Mr. Dix?"

"You got it," Dix replied. "In the movies. In the olden days."

The olden days, Tree thought. Was John Twist in the 1960s now 'the olden days?' For those of a certain age, it seemed so.

"You're sure it's John Twist?" Tree asked out loud.

"You know him?" Shell flared accusatorily, as though it was not a good idea to know John Twist.

"I know him from the movies," Tree replied carefully. "I would think he's a little old to be seducing young women."

"Nonetheless, he is the offender," Shell said in an insistent voice.

"Definitely, the offender," echoed Dix.

Tree glanced at Gladys at her desk, not moving, her face set in a neutral expression.

"And you're sure its Twist who is with April May?" Tree stalling for time, his mind a confusion, leaning toward turning down Shell Dean, but afraid of what he and his echo chamber, Mr. Dix, might do left to their own devices.

"As sure as we are sitting here," Shell replied. "Am I right about that, Mr. Dix?"

"Right as rain, sir," confirmed Dix. He gave Tree a hard look. "What's the matter with you? How many times do we have to repeat ourselves—Twist is the man you're after."

"Now, now, Mr. Dix, let's be patient with Mr. Callister.

We've thrown a lot of information at him in a short period of time."

"Beginning to think the man's deaf—or stupid," Mr. Dix mumbled.

"There you have it, Mr. Callister, the whole, tragic story," Shell said sadly. "You will help us." Not a question or a request. Shell was a man used to getting what he wanted.

"Do you have photos of April?"

Shell gave a nod to Mr. Dix who jumped to his feet to open the attaché case he had brought with him. He moved to Tree's desk and dropped three color photos on it. Tree picked them up. Publicity shots, Tree surmised, showing a blond woman—of course. How could she be anything else?—in youthful flower, elegantly posing in an electric-blue evening gown, grinned invitingly at him. What had to have been the Gold Dust Ranch Casino was in the background.

"That's my April." Shell leaned forward to peer at Tree as he studied the photos. "Looker, wouldn't you say?"

"Beauty for sure." Dix amplified his boss's observation.

"Very attractive," Tree said, his voice neutral. Yes, a beauty, alright. But he wondered what April was doing with a miserable old goat like John Twist? Despite what should otherwise pass as better judgement, his curiosity was piqued.

"Let me poke around and see what I can come up with," he said. As noncommittal as he could manage. He could see Gladys frowning unhappily at her desk. This was not a pair she would choose to get involved with, he imagined. "Where can I get in touch with you?"

Mr. Dix had produced a business card and an elegant black fountain pen. He wrote out a number on the back of the card. "Our cellphone," Dix said, standing and coming forward to hand the card to Tree.

"Call us as soon as you have something," ordered Shell.

"Stay in touch, that's imperative," Dix echoed, keeping his hooded eyes on Tree. A bit intimidating, Tree thought uneasily.

"Aren't you forgetting something Mr. Dix?" Shell's voice caused Dix to loosen his gaze on Tree.

"Never forget anything," Dix said. "Wanted to make sure we are all on the same page. We're on the same page, right Mr. Callister?"

Without waiting for an answer, Dix reached into his suit jacket and withdrew a white envelope and placed it on the desk beside the photos.

"And what is in that envelope, Mr. Dix?" asked Shell.

"Three thousand dollars, more than enough to get our Mr. Callister started on his search."

"There you go, Mr. Callister. How about it? That enough?"

"I would say so," Tree said noncommittally. Over at her desk, Gladys looked a lot more interested than she had a moment before.

"Good money," agreed Shell. "In return, we expect results. Right Mr. Dix?"

"You got that right. Results," Dix said darkly. "We want this over and done with so we can get back to more lucrative pursuits."

"You got that right, Mr. Dix—as usual." Shell was on his feet. "Good day to you, sir." He tipped his hat at Gladys. "Your assistance has been much appreciated, ma'am."

"Glad I could help," Gladys said.

Tree watched the two depart, one rake-thin and coiled tight, exuding a sense of controlled menace, the other smaller and chubbier, suggesting a good time. He suspected Shell's manner was a mask hiding someone possibly more dangerous than Mr. Dix. Not a healthy combination any way you looked at it. He rose from his desk, past the immobile Gladys, trailed them through the Cattle Dock Company's retail space. Beyond the open archway, Tree could see Shell remove his Stetson before getting in the back of the white Hummer while Mr. Dix positioned himself behind the wheel. The bodyguard and his client? Or something much more, Tree mused as they drove off. Why was he not surprised that those two were riding in a Hummer?

Gladys had already taken control of the envelope full of cash by the time Tree got back. She was at her desk holding April's photo. "I haven't been here all that long," she said, getting up to return the photo to his desk. "But I've had enough experience to conclude that every time someone plops an envelope full of cash down on your desk, a shitload of trouble soon follows." She pointed to the photo. "This has shitload of trouble written all over it."

Tree picked up one of the photos. "You think I'm crazy?"

"I believe that already has been well-established."

"True enough," Tree said, putting the photo aside, "but if I take this, maybe I can keep a lid on it until I can figure out what's going on. Otherwise, these guys are a couple of loose cannons out there, accusing the star of Rex's life. That has the potential to shut down everything real fast."

"Yes, but suppose John Twist really did abduct this woman?" Gladys ventured.

"I may be crazy, as you quite accurately point out, Gladys, but it's hard to believe Twist is in any condition to do much of anything with a young woman."

"Yeah, but then you don't know John Twist."

Tree gave her a look. "And you do." It wasn't a question.

"Let's say it's something I'd rather not talk about," Gladys replied enigmatically.

"Fair enough," Tree said.

"Quickly changing the subject," she went on, "where's Rex? Hanging out with his new pal, Twist?"

"I don't think so," Tree said. "I don't think they're going to be pals."

Gladys gave a knowing nod. "It didn't go well."

"That's probably an understatement," Tree said.

"I'm sorry to hear it, but do you know where Rex is now?"

Tree shook his head. "Rex left the restaurant before I did. I came back hoping he was here."

"Instead, there were two goons in search of a lost love," Gladys said. She put her hand on Tree's arm. "Hey, you'd better find Rex, make sure he's all right."

Tree's cellphone started rumbling. When he opened it, Freddie said, "Come home."

"Is everything all right?"

"Just get here as soon as you can."

6

Rex's SUV was parked in the driveway of the house on Andy Rosse Lane. Tourists wandered along headed for the beach at the end of the lane or for a beer sitting outside at the Mucky Duck. Another sunny day on Captiva Island. Except it wasn't so sunny for Rex. Tree got out of his car, hoping that Rex wasn't inside slitting his wrists.

Rex's wrists appeared to be untouched. He sipped a beer with Freddie down on the terrace dappled in late afternoon sunlight. Tree took in Rex's doleful expression while he kissed Freddie. He gripped Rex's shoulder, as close to intimacy as his old friend would allow. "Are you okay?" The universal needlessly asked, never truthfully answered, question in moments of crisis.

"He's a prick," Rex pronounced.

"No doubt about that," Tree agreed.

"But that's his reputation, isn't it?" asserted Freddie. "It's unfortunate, the way he treated Rex, but I suppose it's hardly a surprise."

She was sitting across from Rex with a glass of sparkling water, dressed in white shorts and a white top with horizontal navy-blue stripes. Her blond hair looked like spun gold in the sunlight.

"He was a bastard when I did that movie, everyone hated him—and goddamn it, I never blew the line."

Freddie and Tree traded quick glances.

"I didn't," Rex mumbled.

"Listen Rex," Freddie said, filling the ensuing silence, leaning forward to touch Rex's arm. "Like I've been telling you, don't let him spoil everything. He's a small part of the series they're making about your life—and it is *your* life not his. He's here for a couple of weeks and then he's gone. Just stay away from him. What do you care how he acts as long as he gets the job done? At the end of it, your life will be on the screen for everyone to see and admire. Who knows where John Twist will be? And who gives a shit?"

"I didn't blow the line," Rex repeated. "The director wanted me to do it over again, a couple of times. No big deal—until that so-and-so makes it one."

Rex looked at his beer as though deciding whether or not to finish it. He glanced at Tree. "What happened after I left?"

"I told him you're a great guy and he's an asshole—and then I left."

Freddie reacted with the eye roll he had become all too accustomed to over the years. "Great," she said. "That's really helpful."

"What else could I say?" protested Tree. "'You're a great guy, John? Keep hammering away at my best friend. And by the way, how would you like another drink?'"

"Still…" Freddie began then waved away the conclusion of the sentence.

"Freddie's right," Rex said. "I'm just going to stay away from the guy. He obviously doesn't want any input from me. And let's face it, you're the third wheel on a movie set if you don't have anything to do."

Rex rose from his chair. "Thanks for providing a shoulder to cry on," he said to Freddie.

"Would you like to stay for dinner?" Freddie asked.

Rex shook his head. "Thanks, but I'm gonna head home. I want to spend some time sitting in the dark, feeling sorry for myself."

On his feet, Tree embraced Rex, who reluctantly accepted the embrace "Hey, I agree with Freddie. You shouldn't let this get you down."

"Too late," Rex said. "Right now, I prefer being miserable."

Freddie wrapped her arms around him. "Love you, you big galoot."

"Your love will sustain me through my time of trouble," Rex said with false cheer.

"That's what I'm here for," Freddie said. "My love is available any time, sweet Rex."

Rex held her at arm's length and looked her in the eye sternly. "I didn't blow the line. I'm a professional."

"I know you are, Rex," Freddie said. "I know…"

Tree walked Rex out to his car. "I'm not going to the set," Rex repeated as he opened the the door of his SUV.

"I think that's wise," Tree said. "Why upset yourself? Any idea when they start shooting?"

"Next week," Rex said. "I want you to go for me. Keep an eye on that bastard and let me know if he's screwing up my life."

"I can't imagine they're going to be happy having me hanging around," Tree said uncertainly.

"I will phone our useless producer and tell him I want you there," Rex said.

"I'm not sure what good it will do, but sure, if I can visit the set, I'll be glad to do it for you."

"Thanks," Rex said. He managed a smile. "Much appreciated. I don't know whether I've mentioned it before, but you're a good friend."

"You may have declared it a time or two over the years. But then you know what I always say."

"No, what is it you say?"

"As good a friend as I may be, you are a heck of a lot better."

"Who said you were a good friend?" Rex said, rolling his eyes.

"No one," Tree replied. "But from time to time I like to kid myself."

"You keep this up, you're going to start me crying."

Dry-eyed, Rex got into his SUV. Tree watched him turn onto Captiva Drive. He went back into the house and poured Freddie a glass of chardonnay. He took it down to the terrace. "I thought you might need this," he said.

"Dr. Callister to the rescue," she said with a smile of thanks, taking the glass from him. "Our boy is pretty upset."

"He sure is."

"Tell me what happened."

"From the get-go Rex seemed unusually nervous about meeting Twist. It was as though he was expecting something. Sure enough. Almost from the moment Twist sat down, he was poking at Rex. I suspect Twist had been drinking before he arrived. As soon as he sat down, he ordered a double Scotch. That didn't help his mood. He seemed to take a certain amount of pleasure in going after Rex about this line he supposedly blew back in the sixties, during the scene they were doing."

"What's amazing is that Twist even remembers all these years later," Freddie said.

"Apparently, he does. With more booze in him, he went on to attack Rex for being a lousy actor, saying it was no wonder he never made it in Hollywood. That was why he ended up as a TV weatherman in Chicago who didn't know anything about the weather either."

"That's true enough," Freddie said. "But that's why people tuned in. They loved the fact that Rex had this irresistible personality, the delightful weatherman who didn't know much more about the weather than they did."

"That's when Rex got up and walked out," Tree said.

"And you stayed?"

"For a couple of minutes more. That's when I delivered the observation I recounted earlier. Just a reminder, that's also when you rolled your eyes."

"Damn right I did," said Freddie. "You were not the last word in diplomacy."

"No, I suppose not," Tree said. "But at least it was accurate. There was absolutely no reason for Twist to carry on the way he did, drunk or sober."

"He certainly managed to wound Rex," Freddie said. "I don't think he likes to be confronted by the reality of his life in Hollywood. Rex prefers to remember sleeping with Joan Crawford and hanging out in Rome with Sinatra and Hemingway. He almost never talks about acting."

"Rex repeated that he's not going to the set."

"Why should he, given the way Twist has treated him," Freddie said.

"He wants me to be there. Make sure they're not screwing up his life."

"Are you going to do that?"

"I guess I'll drop around and see what they're up to," Tree said. "It's what Rex wants."

"Well, stay away from Twist," Freddie said in a warning voice. She finished her chardonnay.

"There's something else I should mention," Tree said.

"Uh-oh," Freddie said, adopting the unhappy, anticipatory expression she had ready any time Tree was about to spring something on her.

"When I got back to the office, there were two men waiting for me."

"That's never a good sign," Freddie said with a certain wariness.

"One of the men said his name was Shell Dean. Shell claims that his fiancée—her name is April May, incidentally—"

"You're kidding." Freddie's unhappiness was replaced with an expression of disbelief.

"Shell says his fiancée has disappeared. He wants me to locate her."

"Okay," Freddie said slowly.

"Shell claims April in fact was abducted—by John Twist."

Freddie regarded Tree with narrowed eyes. "*Our* John Twist?"

"That's what he says. He has learned that Twist is in the area. He believes April is with him."

"What did you tell this guy?"

Tree hesitated, knowing the answer to that question was not going to go down well.

"Tree," Freddie prodded.

"I told Shell I would try to find April." Tree spoke quietly, as though he hoped Freddie might not hear him, and thus he would be spared her displeasure.

That didn't work. Freddie's already narrowed eyes closed momentarily.

"Shell was with a character named Mr. Dix," Tree added hesitantly. "Mr. Dix and Shell did not give me the impression they would like to hear the word 'no.'"

Freddie was shaking her head.

"I thought that if there is anything to their story, it would be better if I was looking into it myself. Otherwise, Shell and Mr. Dix, a couple of loose cannons making all sorts of wild accusations, the next thing you know they would shut down production and that would be the end of Rex's dream."

"Do you think there's anything to what these two characters are alleging?" asked Freddie, all of a sudden businesslike.

Treating a problem in her usual manner—head on.

"I don't know," Tree said. "It's bizarre. But then judging by my lunch encounter with Twist, he's crazy and a drunk, so I suppose anything is possible."

Tree's cellphone began pulsating inside his pocket. He pulled it out and saw that the incoming call was a Los Angeles number. Who would be calling him from Los Angeles? He wondered.

Clay Holbrook was not in Los Angeles. "Tree," he said anxiously, "thanks for picking up. I've got a problem."

"What kind of problem?" The sort of question that historically had always gotten Tree into yet more trouble.

"It's John Twist?"

"What about him?"

Tree could hear Holbrook taking a deep breath before he said, "He's disappeared."

7

"What do you mean, disappeared?" Tree asked.

"As in gone, not around, absent, no idea where the hell he is." There was an edge of anger attached to the overall exasperation in Holbrook's voice.

"He was supposed to meet me and the director, Tak Shindo—a great Japanese director, incidentally—and he never showed up. I went around to the house we've rented for him and he's not there. Look, I am totally unfamiliar with this area. I have no idea where he might have gone. I need your help, Tree."

"How am I supposed to help? I don't have any more idea where he could be than you do."

"You're a private detective, for God's sake." Holbrook was desperate now. "You know the area. I want you to get out there and find him before he gets himself into trouble and this entire production goes down in flames."

Visions flashed in Tree's head of Shell Dean and Mr. Dix with their vengeful hands around Twist's neck.

"Did Twist show up in town with anyone?"

"Not as far as I know," Holbrook answered. "He has a stuntman and stand-in, Bronco Holiday, I believe his name is. He insisted on using Bronco, but I'm not sure he's arrived yet."

"When we were at the Lighthouse, was that the last time you saw him?"

"Yes. When I left, he was at the bar ordering more drinks," Holbrook said. "I tried to talk him into coming with me, but he told me to go to hell."

"So he's out there somewhere, drunk."

"And man, you haven't seen anything until you've seen the great John Twist in full drunk mode. That's why you've got to find him and find him fast."

"All right," Tree said with a heavy sigh. "Let me see what I can do."

"Thank you, Tree." Holbrook sounded relieved for the first time in the call. That's the last thing he should be feeling, Tree thought.

When he got off the phone, Freddie was looking at him in disbelief. "You're out of your mind to get involved," she said.

He was in no position to disagree with her.

————

Tree finally got hold of Gladys an hour later. In the meantime, he kept hoping Clay Holbrook would call back to report John Twist had shown up, drunk but okay. There was no such call.

"I'm sorry, who are we looking for?" Gladys sounded groggy, distracted.

"John Twist. He's gone missing."

"And you're supposed to find him?" Gladys was abruptly more focused.

"I need your help," Tree said. "Put your thinking cap on and come up with a few dives where he might have ended up."

"I don't want to have anything to do with this," Gladys said adamantly, fully awake now.

"Why not?"

"Look, Tree, I'm supposed to be the office receptionist. Answering phones that don't ring. Chasing drunk assholes around Southwest Florida was never part of my job description."

"I understand that, but tonight I'm changing your job description. You are now officially charged with helping me with drunk assholes."

"Thanks a lot," Gladys said.

"Gladys… please."

"I told you I don't want to have anything to do with this guy."

"Listen, those two goons who were in the office earlier," Tree said. "I'm afraid they might have him. God knows what they might do. If anything happens to Twist then the whole production shuts down, and that's the end of Rex's film."

"Shit," Gladys said. "Meet me at the office in an hour."

When Tree arrived at the Cattle Dock Bait Company, Gladys was already there, waiting for him outside in her pickup truck. She rolled down the window as he approached. "Hop in," she said.

He got into the cab. Gladys was wearing jeans, a black T-shirt, and a navy blazer. That meant only one thing. "Are you carrying?" he asked.

"What do you think?" she said, putting the truck into drive and starting off.

"Do you have any idea where we are going?" Tree asked.

"I know exactly where we're going."

"How do you know that?" Tree asked in surprise.

"Because I know him," Gladys said.

"How do you know him?"

Gladys's smile looked particularly inscrutable in the light from oncoming traffic. "Let's just see if my hunch plays out," she said.

They drove along McGregor Boulevard and crossed the Cape Coral Bridge into Cape Coral. Traffic was light at this time of night. Tree wanted to ask again where they were headed, but given Gladys's edgy demeanor, he decided to keep his mouth shut.

It didn't take long before she slowed and then made a quick left into a parking lot adjacent to a rambling rundown bar on the edge of the Caloosahatchee River called the Cotton Blossom. To Tree it looked like a holdover from another era, a time before everything got cleaned up and gentrified, out of place amid the adjacent white condo blocks gleaming in the moonlight.

Tree followed Gladys to the entrance. The percussive beat of the music blaring inside shook the building. She looked at Tree, her face stern. "I don't like that I'm doing this," she said.

"Okay," Tree said uncertainly.

"Let's say I'm doing it for Rex," she said. Before Tree could ask exactly what she was doing for Rex, Gladys yanked open the door and stepped into a wall of ear-piercing music. Tables in the dimly-lit interior were crowded around a jam-packed dance floor. As Tree's eyes adjusted, it became evident that all the dancers were men and that Gladys was about the only woman in the room. John Twist was here? The coins were beginning to drop from Tree's eyes—that is, if Gladys proved to be right.

She wound her way through the crowd toward the back. Through the weaving, sweating bodies pushed together in the heat of a Florida night, a tall man darted away. Tree caught a glimpse of Gladys disappearing after him.

Tree finally broke through the crowd and came out onto a long, grassy slope that ended at the river's edge. The moonlight captured John Twist, an untucked wrinkled linen shirt open to his waist, his big gut heaving, his hair wild. He was being pummeled by two dark-complexioned young men, their na-ked, bronzed torsos shiny with sweat. One of the men punched Twist in the stomach. He dropped to the ground. The other young man promptly kicked him hard.

Tree started down the slope calling out, "Hey!" That failed to stop another kick. Twist rolled onto his back, hands held high to ward off the next blow.

Gladys materialized in front of the two young men. They both glanced up in surprise. One of the young men called something in Spanish.

"No, you've got it wrong," Gladys replied. "*Piérdase*—get lost!"

Both men had thick black hair and chiseled, youthful fea-tures. They could have been brothers, Tree thought fleetingly, and maybe they were—dangerous brothers.

Gladys seemed unfazed. "I'm not going to say it again," she said calmly. "Get away from him."

"Hombre disrespected me," the taller of the two snarled in English. "He wants me to go with him, then he offers a hundred bucks. I am top of the line, lady. I don't work for no hundred bucks."

"Too bad," Gladys said. "Beat it."

"Who do you think you're talking to lady?" The smaller man's handsome face was twisted in fury.

"Who do you think I'm talking to, dickhead? Now back off. Leave him alone!"

Enraged, the young man lunged for Gladys.

Tree wasn't sure if she already had it in her hand or whether she was simply able to produce the taser with lightning-quick speed. Tree thought fleetingly, yes, she was carrying all right. She fired fifty thousand volts of electrical current into her on-coming assailant. He screamed and collapsed to the ground.

The taller man, very scared very suddenly, did not move.

"Tree," Gladys said calmly, "give our friend Twist a hand, will you?"

Tree moved forward as Gladys said to the taller man, "What are you two, brothers?"

The taller man, face blank with fear, nodded.

"Okay, get your brother and get the hell out of my sight."

The taller young man helped his whimpering brother to his feet. Tree reached down to take Twist's arm, but the actor immediately shook it off. "Jesus, leave me alone," he barked in a slurry voice.

"John," Gladys said in a measured tone, "let him help you. We need to get out of here."

Twist, on the ground, was trying to focus. His ashen face lit up suddenly. "Blue? Christ, Blue Streak? Is that you?"

"It's Gladys. Now get up."

"Gladys? You're Gladys?" Twist was staring in disbelief. "Jesus."

This time, Twist allowed Tree to take his arm to get him upright. His craggy face was bruised. Blood was running from his nose. The two brothers who had assaulted Twist had disappeared.

"How did you get here, John?" Gladys asked.

Twist was using his sleeve to wipe away the blood. "Dunno," he mumbled. "Where are we?"

Gladys sighed and said, "Same old, John. Pills and booze. And young guys when the mood strikes you."

She does know him, Tree thought.

"No idea what you're talking about, Blue," Twist mumbled.

"Don't call me Blue!" Gladys said angrily.

"Been a long time," Twist said with a crooked smile.

"Let's get him to my truck," Gladys said to Tree.

"Go to hell, both of you," Twist announced, yanking himself roughly away from Tree. "Leave me alone."

"You asshole," retorted Gladys. "You're coming with us."

Twist stumbled away, tried to go up the slope. Gravity defeated him. The music from inside the Cotton Blossom was like a driving force throwing him back into Tree's arms.

He shook off Tree, staggered off a couple of yards before bending over to vomit on the grass.

Gladys shook her head. "And I thought I had a nice safe job answering phones."

Twist threw up again.

8

Throwing up had the effect of calming Twist, making him docile enough so that they could get him to Gladys's truck. It took the two of them to squeeze him into the back. As soon as that was accomplished, he stretched out and began to snore loudly. As Gladys drove away from the Cotton Blossom, Tree phoned Clay Holbrook. He answered immediately.

"We've got him," Tree said tersely.

"Thank God," breathed Holbrook. "Where was he?"

"In a bar," Tree said without elaboration. "We're on the road now. Where do you want us to take him?"

"The house we've rented for him on Sanibel, I suppose. I was hoping that being on a secluded island would help keep him out of trouble."

"So far that hasn't worked," Tree said mildly.

"Can you take him home? I'll text you the address."

"We're on our way," Tree said with a glance at Gladys.

"Tree, you have no idea how much I appreciate this."

"We'll get him settled tonight," Tree said. "But if this is how he starts out, good luck controlling this guy for the next two weeks."

"He swore to us that he was on the wagon and that he would behave."

"He lied," Tree said.

———

The white-painted frame house stood on stilts just off West

Gulf Drive. That meant they had to maneuver the semicoma-
tose Twist, stinking of booze and vomit, up a set of steep stairs.
This was accomplished with great difficulty. When they finally
got him to the top, amidst a great deal of swearing on Twist's
part, Tree propped him against the wall while Gladys fished in
his pockets and found a housekey.

Inside, they dragged Twist through the darkness as far as
a sofa and dumped him there. He made angry sounds before
throwing back his ravaged head and commencing to snore
again. Gladys found a light switch that bathed a big open room
in light that bounced off floor-to-ceiling windows. Tree was
breathing heavily from the exertions of getting Twist this far.
Gladys had resumed the shaking of her head, an action she
lately employed with regularity. "What a mess," she said staring down at the sweating lump of flesh spread out on the sofa.
"Not exactly our legendary movie star tonight."

"What do you suppose he was doing at the Cotton Blossom?" Tree asked.

"What men who don't like to admit what they really are doing at a place like the Cotton Blossom," Gladys replied. "Back
in the day, John was known to play both sides of the street,
rougher on one side than the other. I would have thought he
was a little old for that by now. I guess not."

Tree glanced around a room anonymously furnished in
tones of pale green and yellow, the sort of catch-all decor for a
place on the island that rented for a lot of money. There was a
galley kitchen and a bedroom off the main room.

"There's something missing here," Tree announced.

Gladys looked at him. "What's that?"

"A woman named April May."

"Ah, yes, the weirdly named April May," said Gladys know-
ingly. "Your new pal Shell will be disappointed."

"I don't think Shell likes to be disappointed," Tree said.

"It does beg the question, if the woman isn't here, where is she?"

"Back in Reno, maybe?"

That drew a noncommittal shrug from Gladys.

From outside, they heard the sound of footsteps coming up the stairs. A moment later, the door opened and a grim Clay Holbrook entered. He wore shorts, a T-shirt, and behind his glasses, a relieved expression. That disappeared as soon as he saw Twist sprawled on the sofa.

"My God," he said, advancing into the room. "What happened to him?"

"He ran into a couple of guys who didn't know he is a movie star," Tree said. "Luckily, I had Gladys along with me. Otherwise, it could have been a lot uglier than it was. I don't think the two of you have met."

Holbrook distractedly shook her hand. "Thanks, Gladys."

"You've got your hands full," Gladys said.

Twist snored louder. Holbrook looked at Tree. "I suppose we'd better try to get him into the bedroom."

With Tree's help, Holbrook managed to move Twist into a sitting position. "John," Holbrook said to him in a loud voice, as though hearing, not booze, was his problem. "John, we're going to lift you up and take you into the bedroom. Okay?"

Twist made incoherent sounds that didn't seem to commit to Holbrook's suggestion one way or the other.

"Come on, let's get him up," Tree said.

Together, they managed to raise Twist to his feet. Gladys stood by, arms folded, her expression disdainful. Twist's legs were like rubber so that he was no help as they half carried, half-dragged the big man into the bedroom. He made more incoherent objections until they finally were able to plop him down on the king-size bed that dominated the bedroom.

"Okay, that's it," announced Holbrook, breathing hard. "That's as far as it goes. Christ! This guy is supposed to be on set first thing this morning."

"You may be disappointed," Tree said.

Holbrook made a face and then left the room. Tree found a duvet in the closet and threw it over Twist who was lying on his stomach. Gladys stood in the doorway. "The good Samaritan," she offered with a tinge of sarcasm.

They went back into the living room. Holbrook was hunched on the sofa, elbows on his knees, staring out at nothing.

"What now?"

"God, I don't know." The producer massaged his temple. "Try and get him to the set tomorrow, I guess."

"When Twist got here are you sure he was alone?" Tree asked. "

"I picked him up at the airport. He was by himself. Bronco Holiday checked in late this afternoon, but I don't think he's met with John yet. Why do you ask?"

"Just curious," Tree said. "I thought when we brought him here, there might be someone waiting. An assistant. Wife. Girl-friend."

"Nothing like that," Holbrook said rising to his feet. "I'm beginning to understand why. He's probably alienated every-one who was ever close to him. Except for Bronco, he appears to have stuck by him. Can't imagine why."

Gladys was looking at her watch. "If there's nothing else, I suggest we get out of here" she said. "I think we could all use some sleep."

"Yes, good idea," agreed Holbrook. "I can't thank the two of you enough. Please, Tree, invoice me for your services, and I'll get you paid."

Tree was about to open his mouth to say it was all right, no invoice required. But Gladys got there ahead of him: "That's fine, Mr. Holbrook. I'll get an invoice off to you in the morning."

They went outside and down the steps. There was a cooling night breeze. A nearly full moon peered from between the palm trees in front of the house. "Paradise," said Holbrook looking up at the moon. "Except if you're in the movie business trying to wrangle a drunk."

"It isn't even the movie business anymore, is it?" argued Tree. "I'm not sure what you call it, but it isn't movies the way I used to know movies."

"Whatever you call it," Holbrook said sadly, "it ain't any fun."

9

Gladys drove Tree back to their office. "Thanks for being there tonight," Tree said to her once she stopped.

"It may be time to change my job description," Gladys said.

Tree grinned and said, "Most office assistants don't carry around tasers, that's for sure."

"It was either that or shoot those two clowns," Gladys said.

"I thought you had a gun," Tree said. "I was surprised you didn't."

"I do have a gun," Gladys replied. "A Sig Sauer P320, if you want to get specific. Nine millimetre. Comes with a seventeen-round magazine, which I like a lot."

"Glad you didn't use it," Tree said. "That would have got pretty messy."

"Have you asked Holbrook about Shell and his friend Mr. Dix?"

"No, and I'm hoping I won't have to. Twist is providing Holbrook with enough trouble as it is."

"What about the missing April May?"

"I'd like to keep quiet about that too. If Twist was with her, he isn't now. And he certainly hasn't kidnapped her. Also, I'm not sure what to make of our clients."

"You mean two suspicious hombres who throw down three thousand dollars so you can find a woman Twist probably never abducted."

"I'm beginning to wonder about that," Tree admitted.

"As well you should."

"Would you like to tell me how you know John Twist?" Tree asked.

"Good night, Mr. Callister," Gladys replied. "I need to go home and get some rest. I have to be in the office fresh as a daisy tomorrow waiting for the phone to ring."

"See you in the morning," Tree said. "And thanks again."

"I should say something like, 'Glad I was there.' But I'm not so I'd better keep my mouth shut and just say good night."

"Good night, Gladys."

As soon as he was out the door, Gladys sped off, as though anxious to get away fast. He could hardly blame her he thought as he got into his car. He kept persuading her to do things she shouldn't be doing—but then she did those things she shouldn't be doing so well.

Freddie was waiting for him when he got home, dressed for bed in the flower-printed black pajamas he very much liked. "You look exhausted she said as he flopped down beside her on the couch.

"I've been out wrestling drunks," Tree explained.

"The legendary John Twist," said Freddie.

"Not much of a legend, I'm afraid."

"But then the legends never are, are they?"

"Maybe Joan of Arc," Tree said.

"Yeah, but they burned her at the stake."

"Well, so far they haven't burned Twist at a stake—but then he's only just arrived on Sanibel."

"Tell me what happened tonight."

"I'm not sure you want to know," Tree said.

"You always say that, and you always tell me."

And he did, filling her in on his arrival with Gladys at the Cotton Blossom—she appeared to know exactly where he was—their confrontation with the two young men in the process of beating up Twist. Gladys's timely intervention with her trusty taser.

"Gladys has a taser?" interrupted Freddie. "I thought she had a gun."

"She has a gun and a taser."

"I don't know quite what to make of that woman," said Freddie.

"Whatever you think of her, Gladys certainly knows how to handle a tight situation. I don't know what would have happened to Twist if she hadn't been there."

"What was he doing at a gay bar?" Freddie asked.

"According to Gladys, he plays both sides of the street."

"I see," Freddie said.

"There were two of them. Brothers. One of the brothers was angry and attacked Twist because Twist had offered him a hundred dollars for sex."

"Not enough in this day and age," Freddie said.

"Apparently not."

"When we got him back to his place, there was no sign of a woman named April May. Clay Holbrook showed up and he said that Twist had arrived at the airport alone."

"And how did Gladys know where to find him?"

"She won't talk about it," Tree said. "But she knew him before in Los Angeles. In fact, Twist recognized her from the old days when she was Blue Streak."

"Interesting," said Freddie noncommittally. "Where does all this leave Rex and his movie?"

"In trouble, if any of this gets out."

"Does anyone care these days what an old movie star is up to in his private life?"

"They might if there are a couple of guys like Shell and Mr. Dix accusing him of abduction. And how about a young man at the Cotton Blossom alleging he was tasered after an encounter with John Twist."

"Poor Rex," Freddie lamented. "I hope this isn't all going to blow up in his face."

"I'm doing my best to stop that from happening," Tree said with more confidence than he was feeling.

"Yes, well, good luck." Freddie didn't seem to buy his show of confidence either.

"Dammit, the earth—the earth! It's beginning to shake ..."

"What?" Tree called down from his perch on the bicycle seat attached to the cross. His arms were aching from being stretched across the crossarm to fit into the fake hands.

"Graves have opened up, the dead are walking!" cried De-Mille. "It's a terrible scene!"

"What are you saying?" Tree called. His arms and hands had become numb. The wig they had made him wear scratched his head.

"React goddamn you!" DeMille yelled, high-pitched, losing patience. "You're dying on the cross for God's sake!"

How were you supposed to look when dying on a cross? Tree had absolutely no idea. He tried a hangdog expression.

"What's he doing?" DeMille demanded of Sal standing nearby.

Sal shrugged. "No idea, chief."

"Jesus Christ," DeMille shouted. "Cut! Cut!" He stormed over to the bottom of the cross. "What do you think you're doing?"

"That is a very good question, Mr. DeMille," Tree answered plaintively. "What am I doing here? My arms are killing me."

"Good!" cried DeMille. "You're Jesus Christ, for God's sake, you're in terrible agony—show it on your face!"

"I thought this was supposed to be a long shot," Tree whined.

"It's what I damned well say it is!" snapped DeMille. He reached up between Tree's legs and squeezed hard.

Tree let out a howl of pain. "Action!" shouted DeMille.

Tree jerked up into a sitting position as Freddie flew into the room. "Tree, what's wrong?"

"Cecil B. DeMille grabbed me by the balls," Tree reported groggily, taking in his surroundings, becoming aware that he was no longer hanging on a cross.

"You were screaming blue murder," Freddie said, her face showing relief. "I thought you were dying in here."

"Well, in a way I was," said Tree, pushing his legs over the side of the bed.

"These crazy dreams of yours," Freddie said.

"It's like I'm there," Tree said.

"Maybe you should see someone," Freddie suggested.

"You think, I'm crazy?"

"Yes, but I'm thinking more about your dreams and maybe doing something to get to the bottom of why you're experiencing them."

"In this case, I think it has something to do with movies." Tree was on his feet now, feeling more awake. "Their past—their uncertain future...I'm not sure."

"Yes, well, speaking of movies in the present, Clay Holbrook called a few minutes ago. He wants you to call him back."

Tree didn't like the sound of that. "Did he say what it's about?"

"Call him," Freddie said.

Tree decided he needed a shower first and some time to get past the fact he wasn't really nailed to a cross. That it was only a dream. Freddie could be right, he thought as he finished his shower and toweled himself off. Maybe he did need help. Possibly he had needed help for the past fifty years or so. Maybe longer.

For instance, he needed his head read for calling Holbrook back. But that's exactly what he did.

"Thanks for calling back, Tree," Holbrook said when he answered his phone.

"What's up?" demanded Tree.

"I need to see you right away. Can you come to the set?"

"What's wrong?" Something had to be wrong.

"Do me a favor will you? Please get over here as fast as you can."

Before Tree could tell him there was no way he was going to the set this morning after what they had been through last night, Holbrook broke off the connection.

10

The film crew had set up for the day's shooting at Bowman's Beach off Sanibel Captiva Road. The parking lot adjacent to the beach was jammed with trailers and equipment trucks so that Tree had to park on the edge of the roadway leading in.

A huge crane hovered over the shore, while crew members maneuvered a small camera on wheels. As was the case on movie sets Tree was on years ago, crew members hovered everywhere. There was always an awful lot of standing around on movie sets, Tree thought. That had not changed from what he could see. Except now, crew members studied their cellphone screens or held the phones attached to earbuds and spoke into them. That was different, Tree thought as he stood at the edge of the beach. But then, he mused, everything was different these days. Everything was changing. Including what passed for a movie. This certainly was not a movie that Cecil B. DeMille would recognize, one that would be shown in vast movie palaces across America. DeMille would never believe that this production was designed not for movie palaces that no longer existed, but for viewing in living rooms across the world. No movie palace necessary. For that matter, no movie palace available. DeMille would be appalled.

Holbrook appeared, his strained face breaking into a weak smile when he spotted Tree. "I was just wondering if you would show up," he said, shaking Tree's hand.

"You sounded pretty frazzled on the phone," Tree said.

"Frazzled. That's a good word for what I'm experiencing," Holbrook said. "It's ten o'clock and we haven't gotten a shot yet. Running behind. This young director, Tak Shindo, I'm not sure about him."

Was any producer ever sure about a director? Tree thought.

"I mean," Holbrook continued, "it's a simple shot, Twist on the beach staring reflectively out at the water, remembering his past. Not sure what the holdup is."

"How's Twist?" Tree asked.

"That's what I need to talk to you about," Holbrook said. "Let's go to my trailer, where it's a little more private."

Tree was about to follow Holbrook, when the producer was interrupted by a short, angry young Asian man, completely bald, wearing cargo shorts. "Clay, have you got a moment?"

"Sure thing, Tak." He indicated Tree. "I'd like you to meet Tree Callister. Tree, this is our fine young director, Tak Shindo."

"Your fine young director is not doing so fine this morning," Shindo grumbled. He did not pay the slightest attention to Tree, but focused on Holbrook.

"What's wrong?" A question that a producer should never ask on a movie set, Tree mused.

"What's always wrong lately," said Shindo. "John goddamn Twist is what's wrong. I just spoke to him. He warns me he only does one take. That's it, he tells me. One take and he walks. I don't do one take, Clay. I do the takes necessary to make a scene work. I can't be held prisoner by this guy."

"I'm on my way to his trailer now." Holbrook spoke reassuringly. "I'll have a talk with him."

"Honestly, I could kill this guy," Shindo said grimly. "I never thought I'd say that about anyone, certainly not an actor. But that's out the window now, and we're just getting started. I could kill Twist."

"You and everyone else," Holbrook said, equally grim.

"Who is this guy? You keep saying he's a bigtime movie star. But I've never heard of him."

"Another era, Tak. Another era. Let me talk to him."

"Please do," Shindo said. "This is unacceptable. I'm not putting up with it." He turned and walked away.

"Christ," Holbrook said under his breath. "Tak and Twist. They're competing for the role of biggest pain in the ass on this movie."

Without waiting for a comment, he marched into the parking lot, Tree following. Holbrook, he noticed, occupied the largest trailer in the lot. A mark of prestige in the strange hierarchy of the movie set? Tree wondered.

The interior was done in warm gray tones. Designed, Tree imagined, to sooth the nerves of overstressed movie people. The colors didn't seem to be working for Holbrook this morning. His jaw was tensely set as he asked Tree, "Would you like something? Coffee?"

"No thanks," Tree said. "I'm fine."

"Sit down, please." Holbrook indicated the sofa. Tree took a seat, watching Holbrook fidget with a coffeemaker on the counter in the tiny kitchen unit. "Did you say you wanted coffee?" he asked distractedly.

"No, I didn't," Tree replied. "Clay, why don't you tell me why I'm here."

Holbrook pushed the coffeemaker to one side. "Yes, sure." He slumped into a chair across from Tree. "After last night, I'm worried about John, you know, keeping track of him."

"I don't blame you," Tree said.

"Thanks to you and your associate, Gladys, we dodged a bullet," Holbrook said.

"For now anyway," Tree cautioned, thinking about Gladys tasing the young man at the Cotton Blossom.

"The next time we may not get off quite so easily. That's why I'd like to hire your detective agency to keep an eye on John for the next two weeks. Make sure he doesn't get into more trouble."

"I'm not sure Twist will like that idea," Tree said. He didn't much like the idea, either. It would be much like trying to keep the bull quiet in the china shop, he mused.

"I don't give a shit what he likes or dislikes," Holbrook said, suddenly angry. "Despite his promises to the contrary, he's putting this whole production in jeopardy. Anything I can do to prevent that is fair game."

"Have you talked to Twist about this?"

"I don't have to talk to him. I'm the boss around here," Holbrook said, sounding a lot more decisive than he had before. "I want this to happen and it will happen."

"Look, I understand the problem you're facing," Tree said. "But I'm not so sure I'm the answer. I doubt he's going to listen to me, or Gladys for that matter, any more than he listens to anyone else."

As he leaned forward, Holbrook's anger was replaced by an expression of desperation. "Given your impressive performance last night, Tree, you are my best hope—my *only* hope when it comes to that—for keeping him out of trouble."

"I don't know," Tree said.

Holbrook leaned in further, closer to Tree, his face even more intense. "I know this production is very important to Rex. I understand that. He's had a tremendous life and I want to do my very best to honor that life. But it all falls apart if we can't control Twist. Don't do this for me or for Twist. Do it for Rex."

Holbrook had a point, Tree had to reluctantly admit to himself. This was all about Rex. "Let me talk to Twist," Tree said.

"Like I said, this is a decision I'm making."

"I know, but I'd still like to talk to Twist first."

Holbrook gave a resigned sigh. "He's in his trailer. I'll go with you."

"No," Tree said. "It's better if I talk to him alone."

———

Holbrook insisted on escorting Tree as far as Twist's trailer. It wasn't as big as Holbrook's, Tree noted. It took a while, with Holbrook pounding on the door, before Twist opened it. "Tree Callister is here," Holbrook said quickly. "He'd like to have a word with you."

Twist looked vaguely surprised. Tree thought for sure he was going to say no. But then he jerked his head up and down and said, "Sure, come on in, Tree."

The interior of Twist's trailer was done in beige tones, not nearly as warm and welcoming as the gray motif in Holbrook's trailer. Twist's size seemed to fill the interior. Despite his overindulgence the night before, he didn't look too much the worse for wear, Tree thought. He was dressed in jeans and a white shirt, untucked as usual to more or less hide his girth. The makeup people had been at him so that he looked tanned and fairly healthy, his mane of white hair combed carefully back.

The air was thick with the stale smell of cigarette smoke. Twist soon added to it by using a Zippo lighter to fire up a cigarette. "What can I do for you?" He leaned against the counter, blowing out smoke. He didn't resemble Rex but he did have a certain presence, Tree had to admit.

"How much do you remember about last night?" Tree asked.

Twist's eyes narrowed suspiciously. "Is this what this is about?"

"How much do you remember?" Tree asked again, insistently.

"Not much, but from what I do remember, I guess I've got you to thank for getting me the hell out of there." Twist didn't sound very enthusiastic, Tree thought. The actor flicked his cigarette in the general direction of a nearby ashtray.

"I've come here this morning to tell you that no one wants that happening again, at least while you're filming on Sanibel," Tree said.

Twist didn't explode, the way Tree might have imagined. Instead, he gave him a sly look. "And how do you intend to do that?"

"By not letting you out of my sight," Tree answered.

Tree braced himself for the explosion he was now certain was about to come. Instead, Twist doused his cigarette in the ashtray and fished another out of a nearby pack.

"You think you can keep me out of trouble?" He smirked as he stuck the cigarette in the corner of his mouth. "No offence, but you don't look like you could keep anyone out of trouble. And let me tell you, friend, I'm a big goddamn mountain to climb when it comes to trouble."

"You're here this morning instead of in a hospital or a jail cell," Tree countered. "I think that says something."

Twist busied himself lighting his cigarette with the Zippo lighter so for a time he didn't respond. "Tell me something," he said. "Was I hallucinating last night or was that Blue Streak with you?"

"As she told you, she now uses her real name, Gladys Demchuk."

"Blue, quite a woman," Twist said dreamily. He jabbed his cigarette in Tree's direction. "Tell you what. You bring Blue along on our merry journey together, and you got yourself a deal."

"Why do you want Gladys?"

"Because," said Twist, breaking into a wide grin. "If I recall rightly, she has a taser, and you don't. What do you say Old Tree?"

"I'll do my best," Tree said. "How do you know her, anyway?"

Twist raised and lowered his eyebrows suggestively. "I guess you'd better ask Blue."

"I have. Gladys doesn't say much."

"Bring her along," Twist said with a grin.

A knock on the door dissolved that grin. "Mr. Twist," a voice called. "They're ready for you on set."

"Shit," Twist mumbled. He stubbed out the cigarette, lifted himself away from the counter, at the same time straightening his shoulders, pushing out his chest, and, as best he could, sucking in his stomach. "Showtime," he announced.

———

The crew had set up their shot at the beach. The director, Tak Shindo, was high in the air atop the crane with the camera operator. Tree watched, amused at the thought that Shindo had no real idea of who Twist had been in his heyday. Generations of movie stars like Twist had been forgotten, even by the people who now made movies.

"Where is he?" Shindo called to no one in particular. At ground level, the first assistant director scurried away, presumably in search of the star. Everyone else remained in place, poised for action.

Tree was standing well back, conscious that a stranger on a movie set was always the intruder who got in the way. Holbrook sidled up to him and made like he was concentrating on the scene at the beach. "How did it go?" he asked out of the corner of his mouth.

"I think we're okay," Tree said.

"He agreed?" Holbrook sounded as much surprised as relieved.

"More or less," Tree said.

"We've got John Twist flying in," announced the first AD as he reappeared on beach. "Let's go people. Let's have quiet on the set!"

Everyone settled. There was movement behind Tree and Holbrook. Tree turned to see Twist come along the pathway onto the beach, trailed by hair and makeup people. Twist paused to take in the scene around him. "Okay," he called out, "let's shoot this turkey!"

Up on the crane, Tak Shindo raised his voice to say, "Everybody, here we go... and... *action!*"

Twist threw his shoulders back, puffed out his chest, and drew in his stomach as he began to walk forward. There was a majesty to that walk, Tree thought. Not a Rex Baxter walk, vintage John Twist. The walk he had employed so effectively over the years, moving down dusty western streets to confront the bad guys at the climax of a dozen films. There were no bad guys today though, although it looked to Tree as if Twist was prepared for them should they make an appearance. He reached the water's edge and came to a stop to look out across the bay as the camera crane swooped down on him and then away again.

"And...cut!" cried Tak Shindo. Everyone relaxed. A murmur went up from the crew. The crane swung down so that the Shindo could lean forward to Twist. "Very good, John. Let's do one more for insurance."

"Okay," called the assistant director, "we're going to go again!"

"No, we're not," said Twist. "You got your shot. That's enough."

Shindo frowned down at Twist. "John, we talked about this—"

"You keep talking, Sak or whatever your name is—I'm walking."

Twist was already turned around and headed off the beach. His walk, Tree noticed, wasn't quite so majestic this time, shoulders slumped, not bothering to hold in his stomach, an old man wanting to get the hell out of there.

"Goddamnit," Holbrook exploded. "This is what we're up against. One take and he's gone." He glared at Tree. "Keep a close eye on that bastard. If he ends up dead, I'm probably the guy who killed him."

Tree watched Shindo, down off the crane, flailing about on the sand in what his mother when he was a kid would have identified as a temper tantrum. The first assistant director, at the same time, was doing his best to hold it in, but he was looking pretty pissed. If Twist was out to alienate everyone he encountered, he was doing a fine job, thought Tree.

11

Rex was not in the office when Tree got back, but Gladys was, sitting rigidly at her desk, looking tense. Tree could understand why as he saw Shell Dean and Mr. Dix seated in front of his desk. Shell brightened when he saw Tree. "We've been waiting for you," he said unnecessarily.

"So I see," said Tree with a glance at Gladys.

"I've been trying to phone you," she said icily.

He had turned his phone off when he arrived on the set.

"Apologies for keeping you waiting," Tree said, slipping behind his desk. He noticed Mr. Dix was glowering. "What can I do for you?"

"We have come to express our disappointment," Shell announced brusquely. "Isn't that so, Mr. Dix?"

"That about sums it up, rightly enough," said Mr. Dix.

"Disappointment?" As though Tree couldn't guess.

"With three thousand dollars warming your pocket," said Mr. Dix in a low growl, "we might have expected to have heard something about John Twist."

"You hit the nail on the head, Mr. Dix." Shell nodded enthusiastically while Mr. Dix continued to scowl.

Shell then addressed Tree. "Sir, although you don't appear to know, Mr. Dix and I have gained information you may find helpful."

"And what information is that?" asked Tree.

"Information that said John Twist is in fact on Sanibel Island."

"He's making a movie out there," added Mr. Dix.

Tree chanced another glance at Gladys. Her face continued to be parked in neutral.

"Are you sure about that?" was all Tree could come up with on short notice.

"Do you not read the local paper, Mr. Callister?" asked Shell.

"On occasion, yes." Tree could sense where this was going. "Then if you had read yesterday's *News-Press*, you would have seen a report that said John Twist is on Sanibel for two weeks making a movie." He looked over at Mr. Dix. "Have I got that right, Mr. Dix?"

"Absolutely right," said Mr. Dix with his authoritative seal of approval.

"Gentlemen, I'm afraid you've got me all wrong," Tree stated with a lot more confidence than he was feeling. "You didn't give me a chance to explain that, in fact, I do know John Twist is here on Sanibel and he is making a movie on the island. Further, I've had a chance to talk to people connected with the production and have it on very good authority that Twist arrived by himself and is alone in the house the production has rented for him."

"What are you saying?" Shell's eyes were narrow slits of suspicion.

"Yeah," chimed in Mr. Dix, his scowl deepening. "What are you saying?"

"I think it's evident what I'm saying. April May is not with John Twist."

"That is not what we want to hear," said Shell decisively.

"What is it you would like to hear?"

Mr. Dix rose to his feet, an intimidating figure, Tree thought fleetingly. "What we'd like you to *do*, Mr. Callister, is get out there and find April. That's what we would like you to... *do*."

"Well put, Mr. Dix." Shell gazed at Tree with mournful eyes. "It looks like you have your marching orders, Mr. Callister." He rose and stood by his associate. "Any questions feel free to get in touch with me or Mr. Dix."

"In the meantime," added Mr. Dix, "we might have a chat with Mr. John Twist ourselves."

"Don't do that," said Tree quickly. Perhaps too quickly. Both men viewed him with looks of surprise.

"Let me deal with this," Tree hurried on. "It's better that way. More discrete."

Pretty lame, Tree thought, but it appeared to satisfy Shell and Mr. Dix. "We appreciate your sensitivity to our situation," Shell said. "We need you to find April, particularly now that we know for certain Twist is in the area. We're willing to give you a chance to handle it your way."

"For now," added Mr. Dix.

"Let's give it a couple of more days," Shell continued. "At which time, we will check back with you."

"At which time we will expect results." The renewed threat contained in Dix's growl was punctuated by a forefinger jabbed in Tree's direction.

And then they were gone.

"That went well," Gladys said dryly. She lifted the Sig Sauer she had been holding in her lap and set it on the desk. Off Tree's unhappy look, she shrugged. "You can never be too careful. Particularly with those two clowns."

He didn't like the idea of guns in the office, but it was hard to argue that when it came to clients like Shell and Mr. Dix, you could never be too careful. He got up and went over to her desk to sit in an adjacent chair so that he was facing her. Gladys frowned. "Uh-oh," she said.

"What do you mean, uh-oh?"

"Whenever you come over and sit by my desk with that sheepish expression, you're about to ask me to do something that doesn't include answering the phone."

"It's John Twist," Tree said.

Gladys's frown deepened.

"Clay Holbrook would like us to keep an eye on Twist while he's here to avoid a repeat of what happened last night."

"Us?" asked Gladys frostily.

"I spoke to Twist this morning…"

"I can't believe he was able to lift his head off a pillow," Gladys said.

"He was on the set, looking amazingly good, actually."

"You spoke to him…"

"Surprisingly, he's willing to let me act as his minder. But there's one thing…"

"What's that?"

"He wants you to be part of it."

"No goddamn way." Gladys, adamant, her frown deepening into anger.

"I am guessing something happened between you two years ago."

"I'm not going to talk about it—and I'm not having anything more to do with that son of a bitch."

Tree, taken aback by the vehemence of Gladys's response, tried another tack. "If you don't do it for me or for Twist, what about Rex?"

"Look, whatever happens, Rex will survive this," Gladys responded. "It's a goddamn movie. It's not like he's undergoing life-or-death open-heart surgery."

"Whatever went down between you and Twist, he remembers you fondly."

"I don't want to hear it," Gladys, snapped. "I don't want

to talk about it." She rose from her desk, gathering up her gun and shoving it into her shoulder bag. "The phones aren't ringing. It's quittn' time here at the ranch. I'm leaving." She got as far as the door before she appeared to have another thought, and turned around to Tree.

"I'll tell you this much," she said. "I came this close to killing him." She shot him a hard look. "Believe me, you don't want me near him."

She marched out the door, brushing past Rex on his way in. He gave Tree a look. "What's that all about?"

"I'm not sure," replied a mystified Tree. "Has she said anything to you about John Twist?"

"Other than to agree with me that he's an asshole, no. But like we talked about, something went down between him and Gladys back in her dark Blue Streak days."

"She's pretty upset," Tree said.

"The way I'm hearing it," Rex said as he made his way to his desk, "he's upsetting everyone. No shortage of people who want to kill him. Metaphorically speaking, of course."

"Yeah," Tree said. "Metaphorically."

Rex made a show off positioning himself on his office chair and opening and closing a couple of desk drawers before he said with studied casualness, "I also hear Clay Holbrook has hired you to nursemaid the boy, try to keep him under control."

"I'm on my way out to his place now," Tree acknowledged. "I was trying to get Gladys to go with me, but she won't go near him."

"Why she stormed out of here, I assume." He stopped opening drawers and looked up at Tree. "When were you planning to tell me?"

"Look, I'm just getting my head around this myself," Tree

explained. "I'm not sure why Twist has agreed to me as his minder, and he's probably not going to listen to me, anyway."

Rex presented Tree with a mystified expression. "How you allow yourself to get into these messes could take up hours and hours on a psychiatrist's couch—that is if psychiatrists still employ couches."

"I thought you don't believe in psychiatrists."

"I don't," Rex said. "But for you, I would make an exception."

Feet-on-the-ground Rex Baxter thought he needed help. That should tell him something, Tree thought.

But what?

12

I'm on my way out to Sanibel to meet him now," Tree said to Freddie, speaking into his hands-free phone.

"Is Gladys with you?" Freddie asked.

"Gladys has opted out of this," Tree said.

"That's interesting. Did she say why?"

"Won't talk about it, other than to admit that in Los Angeles she came close to killing him."

"Maybe it's just as well you didn't bring her along," Freddie said.

"We'll see."

"Tree," Freddie said, her voice tensing, "I know I've said this to you a million times—"

"Don't worry," Tree interjected. "I'll be careful."

"I *do* worry, she said. "I worry because you're never careful."

"I don't think John Twist poses much of a threat," Tree said reassuringly. "Except maybe to himself—which is why I'm here." Neglecting to point out the possible looming menace provided by Shell and Mr. Dix.

"Keep in touch," Freddie said. "And remember—"

"That you love me?"

"No, silly, remember to get a quart of milk on your way home."

Freddie broke off the call. Tree sighed as he drove across the causeway. The life of a private detective, he thought. Danger around every corner, but don't forget a quart of milk on the way home. The old private detective on the job. Too old for this.

Tree slowed to turn into the driveway to Twist's stilted house off West Gulf. Before he could do that, a Range Rover swept past him onto the road. Tree caught a glimpse of a profile behind the wheel, a straw hat pulled low over the driver's eyes. That brief profile looked as though it belonged to John Twist. He swept past Tree in the opposite direction. What was this all about? Tree wondered. Where was Twist going alone at this time of night when he was supposed to be waiting for the arrival of his minder?

Well, he was Twist's minder, wasn't he? And here was the guy he was supposed to mind driving away. The minder, minding—and curious as to where a man new to the area with no knowledge of it might be headed. Back to the Cotton Blossom? He seemed to be able to find that easily enough. Tree turned his car around and set out after Twist's fading taillights.

Twist came onto Periwinkle, following it until he turned left onto the Causeway Road and crossed over to continue on McGregor Boulevard until he reached the Cape Coral turnoff.

Tree caught up with him on the Cape Coral Bridge, wondering if he really might be headed back to the Cotton Blossom. If that was the case, what the hell was he going to do without Gladys and her taser? The old private detective. The helpless private detective. What was the old and helpless detective doing out here in the night? A question he had asked himself a million times during a million nights in the years since he and Freddie arrived in Florida.

The endless question for which, right now, there was no answer because Twist, to Tree's relief, didn't go to the Cotton Blossom. Instead, the Range Rover drove on Cape Coral Bridge Road which soon became, for reasons known only to the city fathers, Cape Coral Parkway. Twist turned left onto a parkway that took Tree to a marina.

With its rows of pleasure boats, their hulls gleaming beneath a nearly full moon, this particular marina resembled all the other marinas that dotted the shoreline along the Caloosahatchee River. What stood out, Tree saw after he parked his car, was the fifty-seven-foot yacht at the end of one of the docks.

By the time Tree drove into the parking lot and spotted the Range Rover, Twist was gone. Tree got out, thinking he'd lost him. But then he spotted Twist's shadowy figure as it slipped along the dock toward the big white yacht with a mounted flybridge. Tree saw him climb the stairway to the yacht's aft deck.

It was deathly quiet save for the creak and sway of dozens of boats restless in their berths as Tree crept along past teak-inlaid stairs to the stern. *Black Marlin* was in swirling letters across the transom. He paused to listen for sounds coming from onboard. Nothing except the soft bumping of boats against their protective fenders. He spotted a figure at the far end of the dock. He crouched down, but there was really no hiding place.

Except—a ladder that descended into the water a few feet away at the end of the dock. He crawled forward, praying he would not be spotted in the darkness by the approaching figure. Reaching the ladder, he twisted around so that he could climb down into the warm waters, mostly out of sight but still with a view of the dock. The dark figure reached the yacht's steps. Tree could see Gladys Demchuk go up onto the deck.

As soon as she was out of sight, Tree pulled himself up the ladder, out of the water. Soaking wet, crouching, he ran along the dock back to the parking lot and the welcoming cover of darkness.

He waited for the next hour, shivering as the shriek of the wind rose around him, shutting out ambient sounds. He debated what to do—trying to think of what Gladys was up to, meeting with the man she had refused to go near a few hours before. Should he go aboard and confront the two of them? He was debating that with himself when he spotted movement on the dock. He fell further back into the shadows so that Gladys, in a great hurry, did not see him. She hurried past and disappeared. Soon, he heard an engine starting up.

He waited more minutes to see if Twist followed Gladys. When he didn't, Tree ventured back along the dock. He hesitated at the bottom of the stairs, nervous about what he might encounter if he went on board. A very pissed-off movie star was one possibility. To hell with it, he thought. He was supposed to be minding this guy. Going onto the yacht was part of the minding.

That is what he told himself.

The teak deck was deserted when he stepped onto it, the silence ominous. Not far away, an open doorway cast a pale light emanating from the *Black Marlin's* salon. Tree called, "John? John Twist. It's Tree Callister? I'm coming in."

There was no answer. Tree did not like this. He liked even less the possibilities associated with entering the salon. Easier to turn around and leave. Forget about all of this. Easier but…

He started into the salon.

The woman lay on her back on the floor between a white sofa and a coffee table. She had been shot in the head. There was no doubt, based on the photograph he had seen of her, that this was April May, Shell Dean's beloved fiancée.

A staircase at the end of the salon led down to a dimly lit full-beam bedroom. John Twist was propped in an armchair. His hat lay on the floor. His head was thrown back. Most of his face was a bloody mess. He had been shot a number of times. Whoever did this was not leaving anything to chance.

13

Tree stared at what he could see of Twist in the uncertain light, swallowing the bile choking his mouth. His mind was a hodgepodge of conflicting impulses. The rational part told him to take lots of deep calming breaths and then pull out his cellphone and call the police. The irrational part ordered him to get the hell out of there.

Getting out was probably better, he decided quickly. Calling the police and getting himself—not to mention Gladys—into a lot of hot water before he'd had a chance to sort things out, that didn't make sense. That's what he was rationalizing with himself. The thing he should not do, was the thing he should do.

He backed out of the bedroom slowly, thinking: Did I touch anything? The door into the bedroom was already open so he hadn't touched the handles. The same was true for the door to the salon containing April's body.

Back on the deck, he tore off his water-soaked jersey and used it to wipe down the railing along the transom and then the railing on the yacht steps as he made his way down to the dock. There was no one in sight as he struggled into his wet jersey and then hurried off the dock to his car. Behind the wheel, he started the engine, and then drove away from the marina.

———

It was after midnight by the time he got back to Andy Rosse Lane, dead tired and, if he was being honest with himself, scared. He had just left the scene of a double homicide where he had witnessed the former Blue Streak also make a fast escape after—what? Murdering Twist and his lover? In revenge for something Twist had done to her years ago in Los Angeles?

Yes, that was a possibility, all right. But then he quickly forced himself to dismiss the notion. He would not allow his mind to go toward Gladys as a killer. Not yet, anyway.

For now, he had to figure out what to tell Freddie. Or not to tell her…

Thankfully, she was in bed when he entered the house. He stripped off his wet clothes in the laundry room and buried them in the laundry basket before entering the bedroom and slipping into bed beside his sleeping wife. She stirred a bit before snuggling against him. "You're naked," she murmured.

"Yes," he said. He held her close to him, feeling the warmth of her transfer itself to his cold, naked body. Holding her like this, there was some hope. Not much, but some.

What was he going to do?

Hopeless…

He eagerly kissed her lips, as though kissing her would give him much-needed hope. It worked. She responded as eagerly. Maybe there was some hope after all. She positioned herself on top of him and so yes, he thought, yes there was hope after all, here in this bed with this incredible woman.

The hope that overwhelmed hopelessness. The best hope of all…

––––––––––

"Hopeless?" Cecil B. DeMille said. "No, no, I don't want hopeless. I want you to reflect the hope—the *light* of the world."

DeMille was atop the ladder close to the cross.

"You said this was a long shot, that no one would see my face," moaned Tree. "Now you want me to reflect the light of the world. I don't know how to do that."

"Why not?" demanded DeMille. "You're a Jesuit priest, for God's sake. You're supposed to bring hope to people—light up their lives."

"But I'm not a priest, I'm a troubled man on the run," Tree said plaintively. "It's all hopeless. I can't help myself, let alone light up the world."

"I have to tell you young man," lamented DeMille, "you are big disappointment for me."

"I disappoint everyone," Tree said. "I let everyone down."

"You have certainly let down all of us here making the greatest story ever told," DeMille said. He began to climb down the ladder.

"Hey," Tree called in a strained voice. "Don't just leave me hanging here."

"I do believe I will," DeMille said, reaching the floor. "It will do you good to stay nailed to the cross contemplating the mess you've made of your life and how it is that you are in the predicament you're in."

"No," cried Tree. "I don't want to be nailed to a cross—I don't want to be here. I'm not the light of the world. I can't act! I can't be here…!"

"Tree, Tree…wake up …. Tree…" Tree jerked his eyes open. Freddie's concerned face floated above him.

"Where am I?" he asked in a daze.

"You're in your own bedroom," Freddie said quietly. She ran a hand gently across his face. "I do believe you're a troubled soul these days."

"I'm fine," Tree asserted, swinging his legs over the side of the bed. "I was with this beautiful woman last night." He smiled at Freddie. "In fact, now that I think about it, she looked a lot like you."

"For your sake, that had better be the case."

Freddie rose from the bed and stood back, eyeing him with a doubtful expression. "What happened last night?"

"For one thing, this beautiful woman I've been talking about, seduced me."

"No, before that. Before you got home. Come on, Tree, tell me."

God, he thought, last night. What could he tell her about last night?

"Did you meet with John Twist?"

"No," Tree said vaguely.

"No?"

"He... he wasn't there when I got to his house." A statement that at least nudged at the truth, Tree thought.

"Then what did you do? Why were you so late?"

He wanted to tell her that he had followed Twist to a yacht in Cape Coral. He wanted to tell her he found Twist and the missing April May shot to death. He wanted to tell her all that. He wanted to tell her about Gladys, his desperation, his uncertainty about what to do next, the terrible mess he now found himself in...

Instead, he said, "I drove around looking for him, went back to the Cotton Blossom but he wasn't there." He might have done that, he told himself. If things had worked out differently that's exactly what he would have done.

"Not a good start to your new calling as bodyguard to the stars," Freddie opined.

"No," Tree said. "It's difficult when you can't find the body that needs guarding." Or when you do, he thought, and the body is dead. "I'd better get to the office and check on him."

Freddie bent down, holding his face in her hands while she kissed him. "Are you sure you're all right?"

"A little anxious, that's all," Tree said. "I'll feel better once I know Twist is all right." Knowing full well, he was not all right. Would never again be all right.

Beneath a hot, reviving shower, Tree drew more deep breaths to persuade himself that he had done the right thing in not telling everything to Freddie. More lies of omission, he had to admit. Their marriage had been littered with them, thanks to his insistence at trying to be something he should never have been in the first place—a private detective.

It was ridiculous that he had ever set out on this path that could well lead to a life in prison. Would Freddie come to visit after she realized he had not been honest with her? Who could blame her if she decided not to have anything more to do with him?

Once he was out of the shower and dressed, Freddie had coffee ready for him when he entered the kitchen. WGCU radio played on the Google home mini. As Tree sipped his coffee and Freddie went to take her shower, the local news led with a story about a bill that the Florida Legislature was pushing through that would loosen state gun laws. Another black panther had been hit and killed near Everglades City. There were new concerns about water levels on Lake Okeechobee. There was nothing, as Tree listened intently, about a double murder on a yacht in Cape Coral, one of the victims being the veteran Hollywood movie star, John Twist.

Not a word.

There was still no news as Tree drove down Sanibel Captiva Road, trying to decide what to say to Gladys once he reached the office. *Good morning, I saw you at a yacht last night where there were two dead people. Care to tell me what happened?*

That didn't sound right.

But then nothing he could say would sound right. Their silence made them both complicit in the murders. And maybe Gladys was more than complicit. Obliterating that movie star face as an act of revenge.

As he crossed the causeway, Tree worked to dismiss such wild thoughts. It was one thing to be tough with a gun—and Gladys was—but it was a whole other thing to use that gun to shoot someone in cold blood.

He was spared, for the time being, of having to confront her by the fact that she wasn't in the office. He didn't know whether to be relieved or worried. Was she on the run? Had she decided that, after last night, the best thing was to get out of town?

He was considering this when Rex came in. "I thought you were minding John Twist," he said.

How was he supposed to respond? "I'm on my way over to the set now," Tree said. "Do you know where they're shooting?"

"Don't you know?" Rex asked suspiciously.

"It was a late night."

"Not much of a minder, if you want my opinion."

If only he knew thought Tree.

"I hear they're filming over at Jerry's Foods," Rex said. "I guess they need footage of my character shopping for groceries."

"I'll pop over there and see how Twist is doing." Tree trying to sound casual, feeling tense and on edge.

Rex wasn't to be fooled. "What's wrong?"

"Nothing," Tree said quickly. "What makes you think anything's wrong?"

"You seem tense and distracted."

"Not at all," Tree replied breezily. Or what he hoped was breezily.

"Have you seen Gladys this morning?" Rex asked, thankfully, as far as Tree was concerned, changing the subject.

"Not so far," Tree said.

"Does that woman ever come in on time? It's past ten."

"She'll be in," Tree said.

"I've called her cell a couple of times. She's not picking up."

"I'll have a word with her," Tree said.

"I don't know why I find it so damned hard to talk to her."

"I know you do," Tree said.

"She doesn't give a damn," Rex said.

"That's not true."

"Gladys cares, you're not uptight, and it's a wonderful world," Rex said morosely.

"Something like that," Tree said, no more convinced of those truths than was Rex. But for now, he decided as he left, he would stick with the lie. Hard truths would raise their ugly heads soon enough.

As soon as he reached the movie set, in fact.

———

As Tree came along Periwinkle Way, WGCU still wasn't reporting anything about murders in Cape Coral. He wasn't sure which was worse: the news confirming he was in a shitload of trouble or no news leaving him free to fret about when he would be in a shitload of trouble.

The parking lot, as it was on Bowman's Beach, was jampacked with trailers and equipment trucks, the travelling road show of a movie production. Tree followed a tangle of thick cables up the steps to the terrace that led into Jerry's. Crew members were moving big lights into the supermarket. Tree stopped to allow them to pass. As he did, someone brushed past him.

He turned to see John Twist lighting a cigarette. When he saw Tree, he took a drag and said, "Hey there, Old Tree. Where the hell have you been?"

14

Amid his shock, Tree couldn't help noticing that John Twist looked ... *healthy.* His eyes were clear. His skin didn't quite glow but it was close enough. And he looked rested. "What's the matter with you?" Twist demanded, seeing the look on Tree's face.

"Nothing ..." Tree managed. "Good to see you ..."

"I thought you were coming over to the house," Twist was saying. "Where were you?"

"I ...came over..." Tree could barely get the words out. "I didn't think you were there."

"Waited all night for you, didn't move," Twist said. "Got a damn good night's sleep for a change." He slapped Tree on the arm. "See the effect you're having on me, Callister? Even the thought of you showing up keeps me in line."

He slapped Tree on the arm again. "I'm about to go on set, but come to my trailer later. We'll talk."

He sauntered away into the store, that familiar rolling John Twist walk, leaving Tree numb with shock and confusion. If John Twist was here this morning, bright-eyed and bushy-tailed, then who was that on the yacht last night?

Clay Holbrook appeared. He broke into a wide grin as soon as he saw Tree. "There you are." He came over and shook Tree's hand. "I don't know what you said to John last night, but he's like a new man this morning."

He too slapped Tree's arm. What was this? Tree thought irritably. Arm-slapping day on the set?

"I think he likes you, Tree."

There was no reason in the world why Twist should like him. What was going on? None of it made sense. An assistant director appeared calling for quiet on the set. From inside Jerry's, Tree could hear Tak Shindo loudly call for "Action." Tree edged up to the doorway and peered in. There was Twist, as big as life, at a checkout counter, taking groceries out of a shopping cart with the cameras rolling, and a hundred crew members watching closely.

"...And cut," said Shindo, jumping up to approach Twist.

"John," he spoke hesitantly, "I'd like you to take the groceries out a little slower. You're lost in thought, thinking about your past, how much has changed in your life."

"I'm always goddamn thinking about my past," Twist said. Then, to Tree's surprise, and undoubtedly to the surprise of everyone on the set, Twist winked and said, "Sure thing, Tak. A little slower next time."

John Twist very much alive and shooting a movie, cooperative, and doing a great imitation of a nice guy. What the hell? Tree thought. Something was very wrong. Whatever it was, whatever he had seen the night before that he had not actually seen, he had better figure it out.

He followed the lines of cable back into the parking lot and got in his car. He extracted his cellphone and poked out Gladys's number. There was no answer. He called the office. After a while, Rex came on the line. "I shouldn't have to be answering the goddamn phone," he said grumpily.

"Which means Gladys hasn't come in," Tree said.

"That's exactly what it means. She's not answering her cell either."

"I know," Tree said. "I just tried."

"Where are you?"

"I'm at Jerry's."

"How are they doing?"

"Just fine. Twist is chipper and sober and being cooperative as all get out. My new pal."

"Great," Rex said. "Maybe we'll get my life story on film after all."

Yes, thought Tree after he hung up. Maybe they would—unless he opened his mouth and started asking questions about what he had witnessed last night. Then everything would shut down and that would be the end of Rex's life story on film.

There was only one thing to do—the thing, if he listened to all the cliches on the subject, he should never do—return to the scene of the crime.

The marina was as quiet under a cloudless blue morning sky as it had been in the middle of the night. What was it about these places, Tree mused as he parked his car. Florida marinas were packed with neat rows of pleasure craft their owners seemed to take no pleasure in. If they did provide pleasure, it was at a distance, parked at a marina.

Whether well-to-do people take pleasure in the boats they never use should have been the last thing he was thinking about, he decided. He should be worrying that at any time police would leap out from their hiding places and arrest him for his role in two murders. That's what happened when you returned to the crime scene, was it not?

A potential big mistake, except as he came onto the dock, he saw that something was missing—the crime scene. The fifty-seven-foot, you-can't-miss-it yacht *Black Marlin* was gone from its mooring. He blinked a couple of times and refocused. In the harsh brightness of the morning, maybe he wasn't seeing things properly. No, he decided, he was seeing just fine. *Black Marlin* was no longer there.

Nearby, though, on a much smaller craft, *Archer*, a slim, fortyish blond-haired woman in an orange bikini was sunning herself on the aft deck.

"Good morning," Tree called to her. The woman, sat up enough so that she could remove her sunglasses in order to give him a lazy, disinterested look. Then she replaced the glasses. Tree wasn't worth the effort.

"I'm wondering if you know what happened to the yacht that was at the end of the dock," Tree asked.

"It left," she said shortly. This time she did not bother either to sit up or remove the glasses.

"Any idea who owns it?"

"Why would you want to know that?" The woman sat up on her elbows, removing her sunglasses so that now Tree could see her pale-blue eyes. Frosted blond hair framed a face that even for lying in the sun, had been carefully made up.

"The *Black Marlin*, isn't it?"

"That's right," the woman acknowledged.

"I saw it here the other day," Tree said quickly. "I might be interested in buying it—that is if it's for sale."

"I wouldn't know about that." The young woman sat up further. "No offence, but you don't look like a yacht kind of guy."

"I'm not," Tree agreed. "But my wife is a yacht person. Driving me crazy about it."

"I don't know if it's a good idea to get involved with those two characters."

"Characters?"

"Shell and his pal, Dix. I believe Shell is the actual owner of the boat. A couple of mysterious weirdos, if you want my opinion. Shell's fiancée is a bit cuckoo herself. They don't strike me as yacht people, either. But there you go. You just never know, I guess."

"In Florida, that's for sure," Tree agreed. "Mind if I ask what makes them so mysterious?"

The young woman shrugged. "April, Shell's fiancée, is usually around, but the other two come and go at all hours of the night. Usually their boat never moves, but then they took off early this morning. At least I imagine it was Shell and Dix, along with April. I just got here so I didn't actually seem them."

"Any idea where they might have gone?"

"Are you kidding?" The young woman shook her head. "That's what makes them mysterious—also unfriendly. They're not exactly taking part in our community barbecues."

"Then I guess you don't know when they might be back."

"Or even if they will be back," she added. "Who knows with those guys? I'd look for another boat, if I were you."

"I guess you're right," Tree said. "Thanks for your help."

"No problem." She replaced the sunglasses and settled down again. Tree turned to go as a giant of a man in a crew cut came ambling along the dock. Tree guessed he must be somewhere around six feet, seven inches tall. "Hey, there," he called to Tree, in a friendly voice. "What can I do for you, pal?" He blocked Tree's path.

"You can't do anything for me," Tree said. "Oh, sorry. I do know what you can do. You can get out of my way."

"Funny guy, huh? What were you doing talking to my wife?" The giant wore a short-sleeve Polo shirt beneath which his muscles seemed to ripple with tension.

"What I was doing, I was talking to your wife."

Tree noticed the giant's ham-like fists beginning to curl. "Big Lenny." His wife was sitting up again, taking off her dark glasses. "Lay off. This gentleman was inquiring about the *Black Marlin,* that's all."

"That's some boat. Fifty-seven-footer. Italian design." Lenny's eyes narrowed. "Why would you be asking about the *Black Marlin*?"

"I saw it the other day," Tree said. "I came back to see if it was for sale."

"You got five million dollars, pal?"

"Not on me."

"For God's sake, Big Lenny, give the poor man a break. Let him pass."

"Big Lenny?" Tree said to the giant. "They call you Big Lenny?"

"You a friend of those two jerks?"

"Don't know them," Tree said.

"I don't like it when strangers talk to my wife," Big Lenny said in a voice that made it sound like nothing good could come from talking to his wife.

"I can see that," Tree acknowledged.

"I guess you're a little old to be coming on to my wife," Big Lenny allowed generously.

"That's me all right," Tree said. "I left my walker by my car."

"Ha. Ha." Big Lenny shifted his gigantic physique to one side so Tree could squeeze past. "No hard feelings, right, buddy?"

"None at all," Tree said.

As he reached the end of the dock, he heard the woman's voice call, "Hey!"

He turned. She was standing alongside Big Lenny, all but lost in his shadow. The sunglasses were still off. "What's your name?"

"Tree," he answered. "Tree Callister."

"Tree," she said, wrinkling her nose slightly. "That's a funny name."

"It is," he agreed.

"I'll remember you, Tree." That came out of Big Lenny like a threat. Tree definitely preferred his wife's tone.

Why had she asked his name? he wondered. Given events lately he could becoming even more paranoid than ever. *Black Marlin* was owned by Shell Dean. That would explain what April was doing onboard. Shell could certainly have killed someone he thought was John Twist when he found him with his fiancée. But would he kill his fiancée too? If he found her on his boat with Twist? Yeah, that was certainly possible.

A Range Rover was parked beside his car. Tree noticed the vanity plate on the back: LENNY1.

He would remember Big Lenny too.

15

John Twist had finished shooting for the day, Tree was told when he got back to Jerry's. He was waiting in his trailer. Impatiently.

Spending time with Twist would mean a fight with himself to resist questioning him about how he came to be alive when Tree could have sworn he was dead. But what choice did her have? He had agreed to babysit, had he not? And if he was ever going to find out what had happened last night, he would have to eventually question Twist. If he wasn't dead on the *Black Marlin* then who was?

He knocked on the trailer door.

"Yeah? Who is it?" called a voice from inside.

"Tree Callister," Tree answered.

"Come on in!"

Tree opened the door and climbed the three steps into the trailer. Twist, wearing nothing but his underpants, lolled in an upholstered chair, a lazy old lion at rest after a day's work. "Where you been Old Tree?" he asked in a laconic voice. "I could have gotten into all sorts of trouble while you were gone."

"It looks like I arrived in the nick of time," Tree said humorously.

"There's soda in the fridge over there, Perrier water, beer if you're so inclined," Twist said with a wave of his hand.

"I'm fine, John," Tree said. "Can I get you something?"

"I'd kill for a Scotch, but I'm hitched to the wagon for the duration. That's why you're here, isn't it? Making sure I stay sober?"

"Well, I—" Tree started nervously, not sure how to respond. "It's all right." He waved dismissively. "Gives me someone to talk to. These days no one wants to have much to do with me."

"I'm sure that's not true," Tree replied, suspecting that it was.

"Take a seat," Twist said. "You can sit there watching me, keep me on the straight and narrow. We can bore each other to death. How's that?"

"Sounds good," Tree said. "How did it go today?" He folded himself onto the sofa so that he faced Twist. The movie star in his underwear, Tree thought. What next?

"How does it go any day. I wander around looking pensive, staring into my past. There's not a lot of dialogue." He appeared to drift off, staring into space, a little lost, Tree thought.

"Movies…" he said. "A lifetime sitting in trailers like this one… waiting. Waiting…At the end, what have you got? Images on a screen. Not even a big screen, anymore. A screen in someone's rec room when they aren't using it for video games or getting up to go to the bathroom."

"You don't sound as though you miss it," Tree said.

"I got old, drunk… stupid. In this business, they can deal with stupid. Hollywood is full of stupid people. It's the old and drunk they can't handle."

"Maybe you're being too hard on yourself."

"That's the other thing about stardom. No matter what, everyone always tells you how great you are. It's all bullshit. You're standing in front of a camera, pretending? That's great? It's not great at all. It's crap."

"You made a lot of movies before you retired." The only response Tree could think of.

The hand wave this time was disdainful. "I didn't retire. Hollywood retired me. That's the way it goes. Happens to everyone—biggest stars, men and women. Women particularly. But men too. So here I am, old, unexpectedly sober, and still sitting in a goddamn trailer waiting for the call to another set—the only difference is this time I've got a minder watching me like a hawk." He sounded a touch hostile, Tree thought.

"I'm not watching you," he said, trying to sound reassuring.

"Yeah, you are. And I'm not sure I like it." The hostility was more evident.

"I thought you said you did," Tree said, treading carefully not sure where this was going.

"Maybe I changed my mind." A kind of darkness had settled over his face.

"Are you okay, John?"

"I'm dandy. Why wouldn't I be. A guy I don't know sitting here, judging me..."

"I'm not judging you," Tree protested.

"Sure you are, just like all these other bastards." Now he was downright angry.

"Okay, I'm upsetting you."

"No, you're not." He paused. "Maybe you are at that. You're an upsetting kind of guy, in case you didn't know it."

"I'll get out of here so you can have some time to yourself," Tree said. He rose from the chair.

"Yeah, why don't you do that?" snarled Twist. "Why don't you get the hell out?"

That was a quick nasty turn, Tree thought. Nice guy John Twist did not stick around for long. The suspicious, angry, paranoid movie star soon resurfaced. No booze needed to push him onto the dark side.

As he left the trailer, and started to close the door, Tree chanced a last glance at Twist. He sat motionless, slumped in his chair, staring straight ahead.

Feeling blindsided, Tree walked back to his car, reminded of what someone had told him years ago when he lived in Los Angeles. Never befriend a movie star. The movie star is never your friend. Movie stars don't have any friends. They have people who serve their needs.

John Twist was the reminder of that. Tree apparently served Twist's needs—but only briefly.

Working to tamp down the irritation he was feeling, he didn't notice Gladys. Without saying anything, she opened the passenger-side door and got in.

Tree slid behind the wheel and closed his door. A pale, tense Gladys said, "Do me a favor, will you? Get us the hell out of here."

Tree nodded and started the engine. "Any particular place you'd like to go?"

"Back to Punta Rassa. That's where my truck is parked."

Once they were on Periwinkle Way, Tree said, "I've been trying to get in touch with you. Are you all right?"

"No, I'm not," she answered. "But I guess you know that."

"Do you want to tell me what's going on, Gladys?"

"Your guess is as good as mine," she said. "Tell me what you know."

"I know that you were at the *Black Marlin* last night. I know there were two dead people onboard. How's that?"

"Yes," she acknowledged, "there were."

"I thought one of them was John Twist," Tree said.

"No." Gladys shook her head vehemently. "It wasn't Twist."

"Given that I was just with him, I've come to the same conclusion. Any idea who it is was?"

"No," Gladys said. "Like you, I followed someone I thought was Twist."

"What were you planning to do?"

"What do you think, Tree?"

"I don't know. You might have followed him to Cape Coral intending to kill him."

Gladys snorted with contemptuous laughter. "Yeah, I guess I might have at that, although age and booze will probably get him first."

"Then what?"

"I went in there, saw the slaughter as you did, and just like you, I got out of there. I wasn't sure who saw me, so I've laid low today in case the police came looking."

"I drove back to the marina," Tree reported. "The yacht was gone. But I did find out who it belongs to—Shell Dean."

"The plot thickens," Gladys said. She didn't sound all that surprised. "The mystery deepens."

Tree swung into Punta Rassa and parked beside Gladys's pickup truck. He looked over at her. Her face was cloaked in darkness, impossible to read. "You're not telling me everything," he stated.

"No?" was Gladys's noncommittal answer.

"For instance, what were you doing following Twist in the first place?"

"Maybe I was curious about what he was up to."

"And what were you were doing at Jerry's? How did you get there?"

"Maybe I wasn't too far away and thought I'd wander over in case I ran into you," Gladys said vaguely.

"That doesn't make a whole lot of sense."

"Right now nothing does," Gladys said.

"What happened between you and Twist?"

She inhaled a deep breath. "What does it matter? Whatever happened was another lifetime ago."

"It might matter a whole lot," Tree replied.

"Like I said a long time ago in a galaxy far, far away." She spoke softly. "I was something else entirely back then. We met at a party. He knew what I was and I suppose that intrigued him. I must have been intrigued right back. John Twist. A lot older than me, but a big star. Right? Those were crazy times anyway. I don't know if you could call it dating, but we went out a couple of times. No big deal. Or so I thought. He was drinking pretty heavily even then. Like a lot of men, he did this Jekyll-Hyde transformation once he started. All sexy charm one minute, this dark monster coming out of his cave the next. He started to scare me. This happened late one night at his place. He got particularly nasty, started calling me really bad names. I tried to leave. That's when he exploded. He hit me hard and then hit me harder and harder. Wouldn't stop hitting me. It's like I brought out all his hatred of women that he had been storing up."

"I'm sorry, Gladys," Tree said.

"Nothing to be sorry about. I don't need anyone feeling sorry for me."

"Tell me what happened. How did you get away?"

She took another deep breath. "Eventually, he passed out. I was on the floor, semi-conscious, but I managed to drag myself out of there, get in my car and drive to a hospital. They treated me for a broken jaw. A concussion. Cracked ribs. They fixed it all up. What they couldn't get at was the emotional damage."

"God, Gladys, I keep saying I'm so sorry because I don't know what else to say."

"I know," Gladys said. "I understand."

"I had no idea…"

"Why should you? It wasn't the first time I got kicked around. He just did it better than the others, and he was a lot more famous."

"What happened after you were treated at hospital?"

"What do you think happened? Not much of anything. Hospital officials called in the police. But along with them came Twist's lawyers, armed with a lot of money. All I had to do was decline to press charges."

"I guess I don't have to ask about the decision you made."

"No, you don't. But the good news, such as it is, I was able to retire from my chosen profession—it was high time, anyway—and open my detective agency in Los Angeles."

"Which is how we met," Tree said.

"Which is how we met, no question, although I wouldn't blame you if you're regretting that meeting about now."

"Are you kidding?" Tree replied quickly. "The number of times you saved me since you got here? And you even answer a telephone from time to time."

"Those are the things in your office that make funny ringing sounds once in a blue moon, are they not?"

They both laughed. She leaned over to give him a hug. "Thanks," she said. "But I suspect we're both in a lot of trouble."

"What's new?" Tree said.

"Want to know what I think?"

"Sure."

"Shell's yacht is at the bottom of the Gulf by now," Gladys said. "Along with the two bodies. I suspect Shell and his pal Dix believe they have killed John Twist—and Shell's lady because they caught her with Twist."

"But what happens when they discover they haven't killed Twist—as they are bound to do?"

"More shit," Gladys said firmly. "Are you ready for that?"

Tree gave her a sorrowful smile. "You'd better keep your taser handy."

"I'm afraid we may need the heavy artillery." She opened

here jacket so that he could see the grip of the gun sticking out of her belt.

"What is that?"

"It's called a gun, Tree. Like I told you before, the SIG Sauer P320."

"You use it to shoot people," Tree said quietly.

"It's also comes in handy when you want to throw a scare into someone." She leaned over and kissed his cheek. "See you at the office."

Tree wanted to say something else. But what? Hey, Gladys, did you use that SIG Sauer of yours to kill two people? But then she was out of the car. He watched her go to her truck and get in. He drove off, asking himself the question he had asked himself far too often these past few years: What have I gotten myself into?

16

"If it wasn't John Twist on that yacht, then who was it?" Tree and Freddie were seated on the terrace, Freddie armed with the fortifying glass of chardonnay that provided her with the intestinal fortitude to hear of her husband's latest misadventures, this one concerning the murdered movie star who turned out not to be murdered.

"That I don't know," Tree admitted, "but someone I thought I followed from Twist's house, someone I thought was him."

"But obviously wasn't," Freddie said.

"No."

Freddie sipped at her wine reflectively. "And you don't believe Gladys is involved?"

Tree shook his head. "I don't know what to think. I told you about Twist beating her years ago. She doesn't want to have anything to do with him, which is understandable. But I still get the feeling she's holding something back, not telling me everything."

"Maybe that she shot the wrong man the other night," Freddie offered.

Yes, Tree allowed himself to admit, that was certainly possible. "Whatever happened, that yacht is gone, the cops haven't shown up at the door," Tree argued. "Twist is working and they are shooting Rex's movie, which is what we've all been working to achieve from the beginning."

"Except you're forgetting there is also a dead woman," said Freddie grimly. "Not to mention the poor guy who was mistaken for John Twist."

"I'm not forgetting. I'm just not sure what to do."

"Here's an original idea for you. How about going to the police?"

"Yeah, but then Rex's movie blows up, Gladys is accused of murder, and I end up in prison as an accessory."

"At some point, you're going to have to tell the authorities what you know," Freddie countered.

"But not right now."

"Then when?"

"As soon as I figure out how to get out of this mess and save Rex's movie."

"I hate to say it," Freddie said with a grimace.

"Say what?"

"Your record for getting out of messes, it's not great."

Tree thought of mounting a counter-argument. Then he decided not to. There wasn't much of an argument to mount.

He was saved from further discussion of his sorry record by his cellphone ringtone. Tree groaned. "I don't want to answer it."

"Given your current circumstances, I think you'd better," Freddie said.

"Where the hell are you?" demanded Clay Holbrook as soon as Tree opened his phone. He was immediately sorry he answered.

"I'm home with my wife."

"You're supposed to be with John," Holbrook said angrily. "Why aren't you?"

"He threw me out of his trailer," Tree said.

"Well, now he's on the phone wondering where you are."

"The guy's crazy," Tree said.

"I don't give a shit what he is." Holbrook practically spat out the words. "He wants to see you."

"Where is he?"

"Right now, he's at home. But he won't be there for long if you don't get over there."

"I'm on my way," said Tree.

Holbrook immediately hung up.

Tree looked at Freddie. "Shit," he said.

"You'd better get over there."

"I want you to do me a big favor," Tree said.

"Tree," Freddie announced in a warning voice, suspecting what was coming, "Don't even think about it."

"Maybe if you're with me, he'll behave," Tree said hopefully.

"I highly doubt it."

"Also, you can help me get more information out of him."

"I highly doubt that, too."

"Let's give it a shot—please." Tree in begging mode, a pathetic sight, he thought, but necessary.

Freddie groaned as she got to her feet. "It's a good thing I love you."

"Don't I know it," Tree said.

"Although I'm in the process of rethinking that statement."

"I'm sorry to hear that."

"However, since the rethinking has been going on for the last thirteen years or so...give me a minute to get changed,"

She started toward their bedroom and then paused. "Let's stop at Publix on the way."

"What do you need at Publix?"

"A bottle of Scotch," Freddie said.

17

Fog had settled in across Sanibel. Twist's rented house on West Gulf Drive was barely visible as they approached. The Florida lair of Count Dracula, Tree thought as he parked in the driveway. Gauzy lights from inside indicated Twist was in residence.

Twist opened the door as they came up the steps. He stood uncertainly on the threshold, wearing cargo shorts and a wrinkled linen shirt unbuttoned to the waist so that his tremendous stomach could not be missed. He looked dull-eyed and disinterested.

"Yeah?" he said. He noticed Freddie. There was a gleam of interest that had not been there a moment ago. "Who do we have here?"

"I thought I'd bring my wife, Freddie, around to meet you," Tree said.

"Sure, the Sanibel Sunset Detective's wife, yeah. Come in. Come on in. The more the merrier."

He stepped aside so that Freddie and Tree could enter. She stopped to shake his hand. "Pleased to meet you, Mr. Twist."

"Mr. Twist." He smiled sardonically. "If you're going to hang around me, it's John."

"Sure, John. I'm a big fan."

"Everyone is—until they get to know me."

"I'm sure that isn't the case," Freddie said with a mischievous smile.

"Just ask your husband." Twist's smile this time wasn't quite so sardonic.

The air was thick with the smell of marijuana as Freddie marched across to set the paper bag she carried on the sideboard. "Tree doesn't drink—at least he doesn't drink anymore," she said, removing a bottle of Oban Scotch and placing it on the sideboard. "But there's no reason why you and I can't have a taste." She turned to Twist. "What do you think, Mr. Twist? Sorry. John."

"Call me any damned thing you like, as long as you're pouring."

"I'll need a couple of glasses."

Twist eyed Tree suspiciously. "This your idea of... minding, Tree?"

"Let me get some glasses," Tree said.

"In the kitchen, over the sink," advised Twist.

By the time Tree came back with two water glasses, Twist had settled onto a sofa, a lot more relaxed. "I take mine neat, sister," he said to Freddie.

"I'm not your sister," Freddie said, splashing generous portions of Scotch into the glasses. "But you can call me Freddie."

"Freddie it is," he said as she handed him a glass. He took a deep swallow. "That's better." He slumped back on the sofa, more relaxed than ever. "Take a load off," he said to Tree. "You can sit here and watch while this lady—Freddie?—and me get to know one another."

"It's Freddie, John." Freddie seated herself beside him. "Short for Fredryka."

"I like it," said Twist. He drank more Scotch.

Freddie raised her glass. "Cheers," she said. They clinked glasses. Tree leaned against the sideboard, watching the two of them. Twist had eyes only for Freddie.

"You're married to this character, are you?"

"For almost twenty years."

"Any chance you'd consider running off with a washed-up old movie star?"

"Well, John," Freddie replied with a twinkle in her eye. "Let's not rush things. We've just met, after all."

"I don't have a lot of time left, I gotta move fast." He glanced at Tree. "Maybe you could help things along, Old Tree, by bringing that bottle over here."

"Old Tree is glad to oblige," Tree said. He poured more liquor into Twist's glass. Twist took a big gulp and threw his head back. "Yeah…" he said.

"How are you enjoying your stay on Sanibel?" Freddie asked. She sipped her drink, barely getting her lips wet, Tree noticed. Twist, meanwhile, had all but finished with his second glass.

"How do I like Sanibel?" He lifted his head up enough to grin lazily at Freddie. "It's goddamn boring is what it is. They roll up the streets at—what?—eight o'clock? Nine at the latest. The restaurants are closed, for God's sake. It's all boring. I'm bored. Everything goddamn bores me."

"I'd better do my best not to be boring," Freddie said.

He gave Freddie a measured, up-and-down look. "I'll just bet you can do that."

"I can try," offered Freddie.

"Now tell me, Freddie, how do you plan on keeping an old varmint like me interested?"

"First of all, I'm going to pour you another drink," Freddie said. She threw a glance at Tree. "That's you're cue to move into action, darling."

Tree poured more Scotch into Twist's empty glass. He leaned back, his eyes heavy-lidded, his belly protuberant. "A good start," proclaimed Twist. "A lovely lady, good booze. Can't beat that."

"No, you can't," Freddie said. She set her glass aside. "Now here's something else that will keep you from getting bored."

"Yeah, what's that?" Twist's drink was half gone.

"You and me talking about Shell Dean," Freddie said.

For a moment, this appeared not to register with Twist. He gave her a fixed, slightly confused smile. "What—"

"You see? It worked, John. You're not bored, are you?" Freddie sat back. "Tell me about Shell Dean."

Twist glared at Tree who, with his arms folded, had repositioned himself at the sideboard. "What is this?" he demanded.

"If I were you, I'd do as the lady asks," Tree said.

"Shell... Jesus..." Twist's head was lolling back against the sofa.

"Shell and his henchman, John, why are they here looking for you?" Freddie asked.

"Looking for me," Twist mumbled. "They're not *looking* for me..."

"What about April May? Is she a friend of yours?"

That got a wispy smile from Twist. "What? Yeah, April... Are you jealous, Freddie?"

"I might be jealous, John," Freddie said. "But I think Shell is pretty angry with you. Am I right about that?"

"Shell, that bastard, he set me up with her, that's what Shell did. I should have known better. But like I think I told your husband, when you're old and stupid..." he allowed the rest of the sentence to drift off. "That's why I sent Bronco to deal with her and Shell."

"Bronco?"

"My man Bronco Holiday, he just got here. He's been my stunt double for years. More than that. Gets me out of the jams you get into when you're old and stupid, like me. Tough hombre. Does it the Bronco Way. He knows how to handle a tight situation."

"What did you do, John?" Freddie was leaning forward again, more intense now. "Did you send Bronco to 'handle' April the other night?"

"Bronco found out where they were..."

"Where did he tell you they were?" Freddie pressed.

"Didn't say. Doesn't say. Keeps me out of it. Said he knew how to deal with it—and he does. Bronco always gets me out. So that's the end of that particular problem. My man..." he said dreamily. "My man, Bronco. Takes care of things for me—the Bronco Way."

"Where is Bronco now?"

"Lying low, the way Bronco does. Hasn't been in touch, but that's okay... things are taken care of. The Bronco Way... love it..."

Tree moved forward to carefully remove the empty glass from Twist's fingers. "More..." he mumbled.

"I think you've had enough," Tree said.

"Go piss up a tree—Tree...Old goddamn Tree..." He actually giggled. "Piss up a ... an *Old Tree*! Get it?"

"Very funny," Tree said. "You are a riot, John, no doubt about that."

"Bad man, that Shell..." Twist was back to mumbling. "Goddamn blackmailing shit...him and April and that bastard, Dix..."

Tree placed Twist's empty glass on the sideboard. Freddie rose from her chair, handing Tree her untouched scotch. "Let's get him into bed."

Together, they managed to hoist a complaining Twist to his feet—complaining but not fighting them as they more or less dragged him into the bedroom and laid him out on the bed.

"Turns out, I'm a lot more cold-blooded than I thought," said Freddie, surveying the sleeping Twist, his great stomach heaving up and down in time with his heavy breathing. "I should be feeling guilty about getting a drunk, drunk, but I'm not."

"I know how you feel," Tree said. "As long as he gets to the set in the morning. Holbrook's going to kill me, otherwise."

"There are any number of people who might kill you, my love," Freddie said, pulling out from the closet the duvet he had used before. "But I highly doubt Holbrook is one of them."

She tossed the duvet over Twist and then spent a moment tucking it in around him so that only his head showed—an old and battered head, Tree couldn't help think. A gargoyle's head.

"Let's get out of here," Freddie said. They reentered the living room. Freddie grabbed what was left of the Scotch. "This way he doesn't wake up in the morning and start drinking."

They went out of the house. The mist had cleared to reveal a cloudless Florida night. They got into the car. Tree started the engine and drove out onto Periwinkle Way. Freddie had remained unexpectantly silent.

"What are you thinking?" he asked.

"That now we know who you found on Shell's yacht."

"Bronco Holiday, Twist's stunt double."

"Who, I assume, looks enough like Twist to be mistaken for him," Freddie said.

"Twist sent Bronco to the yacht to deal with Shell and April."

"Maybe it was Bronco and April who were lovers," Freddie said. "Bronco went there to meet her. Shell and/or Mr. Dix found the two of them together and shot them both."

"Then he and Dix decided to take the *Black Marlin* out into the Gulf where they could ditch the bodies," Tree suggested. "Is there a better way to dispose of bodies with bullet holes in them?"

"Destroying any evidence of a crime," Freddie added.

"But what happens when Shell and Mr. Dix discover that Twist is still alive? If that's the case…"

"He and Dix could still come after John Twist," Freddie said. "And here's something else—kind of scary when you think about it."

"What's that?" Tree asked.

"You might be the one person who can keep him alive. So…"

"So what?"

"We had better go back to his house and make sure he's safe," Freddie said.

"What are we supposed to do? Move in with him? I doubt he'd like that."

"Hide him out in the one place where Shell won't think to look for him."

"Where's that."

"Our house," Freddie said as though that was the most reasonable solution in the world.

"You've got to be kidding," Tree said.

"Give me an alternative solution," Freddie said.

He couldn't think of one. Great, he thought. Just great.

18

There was surprisingly little resistance on Twist's part to being hauled out of bed in the middle of the night, trundled outside and then squeezed into the back of a Mercedes. Filling him full of booze had helped immensely.

Once Freddie and Tree were in the car, there was a debate as to what to do with their passenger.

"Our place, like I suggested," Freddie said. "Who looks for a movie star on Andy Rosse Lane?"

Tree still didn't much like the idea, imagining what Twist would be like when he woke up in the morning. "I'm open to another suggestion," Freddie said.

Yes, but as before, Tree didn't have another suggestion.

"Then it's Andy Rosse Lane," Freddie said. "We are the minders, minding."

———

Back at their place, it took all their straining efforts to extract Twist from the car and then get him into the house, Twist objecting now, mumbling and swearing, but without the strength to do much else.

Finally getting him into bed in the guest room left the two of them exhausted.

"We're getting too old for this," observed Tree.

"We've always been too old for this," replied Freddie as they retreated into their bedroom. "I keep telling myself I'm doing this for Rex. Otherwise, I would kill you."

"Please don't kill me."

"All right. You've talked me out of it—for now."

"We just have to make sure he gets to the set the next couple of weeks and then it's over," Tree said. "Twist can fend for himself back in L.A."

They got into bed. Freddie turned out the light. He drew her to him. "Thank you," he said, holding her tight. She kissed him lightly on the mouth. He drew her closer.

From the other room, they heard screaming. "Good grief," said Freddie, sitting bolt upright.

Twist was yelling something they couldn't quite make out.

Freddie leapt out of bed, Tree following. Entering the darkened guest room, they found Twist flopping around wildly on the bed. "Monster," he shouted. "Monster! Monster!"

Freddie went to him. "John," she called to him. "John…"

He continued to shout "Monster!" as she sat on the edge of the bed holding him. "John, it's all right." She ran a hand gently over his face. Twist settled a bit. His eyes popped wide open, filled with panic. "Where am I?"

"You're with us, John," Freddie said gently. "You were having a bad dream, that's all."

He tried to sit up but couldn't. He lay back, his breath coming in short, loud bursts. "Oh, God," he said. "Oh, God…" Suddenly, he gripped Freddie's arm, lifting himself up, his eyes wilder than ever—filled with fear this time. "So sorry… Please forgive me…Please…sorry…sorry…"

He loosened his grip and fell back on the bed, gasping. Finally, he seemed to settle again, falling back to sleep.

Freddie moved off the bed slowly. "I think he's okay now," she said in a whisper.

They crept out of the room.

"What do you suppose that was all about?" Freddie said.

"Something from his past he's feeling a lot of guilt over, I would say," Tree said.

"What do you think? Gladys?" Freddie asked.

"Maybe," said Tree. "There could be lots of other women as well."

"A haunted old man," Freddie said as she pulled the covers up around them. "Trying to hide his fear and remorse by swaggering around making life miserable for everyone."

"Is that your dime-store analysis?" Tree asked.

"For what it's worth, yeah." She lifted herself up on her elbow for a better view of her husband. "How about you? How are you feeling?"

"Like an old man haunted by his past," Tree said.

"What? Is Twist making you feel pangs of guilt?"

"What do I have to feel guilty about?" As though Tree couldn't spend the rest of the night on that subject.

"How about your three ex-wives? Do you feel guilty about them?"

"It's more like guilt around dragging you into all the trouble I get myself into."

"Interesting," Freddie said noncommittally. "Although I don't hear you screaming out in the middle of the night, begging forgiveness."

"That doesn't mean I don't feel guilty," Tree said.

"I think I've suggested before what you could do about those guilt feelings of yours."

"Remind me again."

"Stop doing what you're doing," Freddie said. "It's as simple as that."

"You know I've tried," Tree protested. "But no matter what, I always seem to get dragged back into it."

"Try harder," Freddie advised.

"You're so mean to me, constantly assaulting me with common sense."

"Guilty as charged. It's one of my many shortcomings."

"You don't have any shortcomings," Tree said, nuzzling against her.

"Good answer," she murmured. "I have a question for you?"

"What's that?"

"What is it you think you're doing?"

"I'm caressing your breasts."

"I thought so," Freddie said.

"Your gorgeous breasts," Tree added. "Demonstrating we're not so old that he can't do this."

"Ah," Freddie said with a moan. "That…"

19

When Tree came in at six the next morning to wake John Twist, he was already in the guest-room shower. He came out of the bathroom a couple of minutes later, a towel fighting hard to hide his immense girth. "You're up," said Tree, unable to hide his surprise.

"Great detective work," Twist said. "Rule number one in this business: No matter what happens the night before, you're up the next morning and on the set for your call time." He paused and gave Tree a bleary look. "What did happen the night before?"

"We've got coffee in the kitchen," Tree said by way of dodging the question.

"Is this your way of saying you don't want to tell me what happened last night?"

"Something like that," Tree said.

Twist gave him a look. "That bad, huh?"

"No, not bad at all. Get dressed and we'll talk."

"He's awake," Tree said to Freddie when he came into the kitchen.

"I'm amazed he's still alive," Freddie said. She was spooning coffee into their coffeemaker.

Tree pulled out his phone and called Clay Holbrook. The producer came on the line immediately. "Tell me you know where Twist is," he blurted.

"He's at my place," Tree said.

"Thank God," Holbrook said, his voice filling with relief. "What kind of shape is he in?"

"He's in the shower, preparing to come to the set," Tree said.

"He's due in an hour. Can you get him here?"

"Where are you?"

"We're at the Lighthouse Restaurant today. In the bar area."

"I'll see you there," Tree said as Twist came into the kitchen, dressed. He brightened when he saw Freddie pouring coffee. "Good morning," she said.

"Freddie. Have I got that right?"

"You do," Freddie said. "Would you like coffee?"

"Black, please," Twist said.

"I just spoke to Holbrook," Tree said. "You're due on set in an hour."

"In the meantime, maybe you can tell me what happened last night. How did I end up here—and come to think of it, where's here?"

"You don't remember anything?" Freddie was pouring coffee.

"My stock in trade," Twist said. "I don't remember. Usually, it's better that way."

Freddie glanced at Tree as she brought the cup over to Twist. "Here, is our home on Captiva Island," she said. "We thought you'd be safer staying with us. Why don't you sit down? Would you like something to eat?"

"I think we'd better get to the set," Tree said.

"I can get some breakfast there," Twist said. He sipped at his coffee. "At least I think they'll give me some breakfast." He drank more coffee and then said, "Tell me why I'm safer here."

"There's a guy named Shell Dean?" Tree said. "You told us about him last night."

"Did I?" Twist was looking at his coffee cup. "That's the trouble when I'm drunk. I say too goddamn much." He paused.

"What did I say?"

"You said he was blackmailing you."

Twist didn't respond immediately. "Did I?" he said carefully.

"He and his associate, Mr. Dix."

Again, Twist seemed in no hurry to answer.

"He owns casinos in Reno, Nevada. You've been there, right?"

"I've got a place out there," Twist conceded.

"He seems to think you stole his fiancée from him."

Twist snorted derisively. "That's bullshit. At my age, I'm past stealing anyone."

"Then why do you suppose he's looking for you?" Tree pressed.

Twist offered a wry grin in response. "It looks as though you've got your work cut out for you, Old Tree, protecting my sorry ass." He looked at his watch. "We'd better get going. Don't want to be late and get a bad reputation." He looked at Freddie and grinned. "Thanks for the coffee."

———

"Fredryka." Twist gave her name a certain eloquence as Tree drove down Sanibel Captiva Road. "I like her." He gave Tree a sideways glance. "You're a lucky man, my friend."

"Yeah, I am," Tree agreed. "What about you? No one in your life?"

"Ha," came out as an explosion of air. "Like I said back there, I'm past stealing women. I'm also past marrying them. Five tries and a fortune later, I've stopped trying. Or—" he added as an afterthought—"as you saw the other night, I can play for the home team from time to time. It's easier. Usually."

He cast a glance at Tree. "What about you?"

"What about me?"

"I get the impression Freddie's not your first wife."

"It took me three tries before I got it right."

"You've been married four times?" Twist sounded impressed.

"That surprises you?"

"A little bit, yeah, you don't seem like a four-times kind of guy."

"No?"

"More like the solid married-man type."

"I'm afraid Freddie might disagree with you."

"You don't drink. You don't smoke. You just get into a lot of shit with guys like me. Right?"

"Something like that," Tree agreed.

"Blue Streak." Twist didn't say her name with quite so much eloquence.

"You mean Gladys. What about her?"

"Where does Blue fit in to all this?"

That came out of left field, Tree thought. "She is Gladys now," he reminded.

"Okay. Gladys."

"She answers the phone in the office and does her best to keep me out of trouble. Why do you ask?"

"Let's say we were acquainted back in the day. I'd like to get together with her." He gave Tree another sideways glance. "Do you suppose you could arrange that?"

"I'm not so sure she wants to see you, John." No use beating around the bush, Tree thought. Gladys was adamant about staying away from him after what he did to her.

"I see," was all Twist replied.

"You don't remember what happened?" Tree ventured.

"Nothing happened," Twist replied quickly.

"She—" Tree began.

Twist cut it off. "Let's leave it at that. Okay?"

Tree didn't say anything else. Approaching the causeway, an uneasy silence descended. It was another perfect, cloudless Florida day. White pelicans swooped and soared in the bright sun above the causeway. More pelicans were lined up along the railing. A power boat left a gleaming wake as it sped across the calm waters of San Carlos Bay. A morning like this should produce a sense of well-being, Tree reflected. But this morning he felt nothing like well-being. He was tense and stressed as Twist shifted uncomfortably beside him.

"Good things. Bad things. All things," Twist muttered, breaking the silence. "What you choose to forget in a lifetime." He squirmed some more. "But I have nothing but fond memories of our time together." He was speaking in a formal voice, as though answering an interviewer's question. Which, in a way, he was.

"Gladys doesn't see it the same way," Tree offered tentatively, uncertain how far to push.

"Do me a favor, will you? Whatever happened, well…" He stopped, seeming at a loss for what to say next. He shook his head. "See what you can do to set up a meeting between the two of us, okay?"

"I'll talk to her," Tree allowed. "But I wouldn't hold my breath."

"Do your best," Twist said. He stared out at the bay.

By now, Tree was used to the sight of parking lots filled with trailers and camera trucks. This morning was no different, as he pulled into the Lighthouse Restaurant and stopped to let Twist off.

He opened passenger door and started out, then paused

and turned to Tree, his eyes narrowing suspiciously. "I'd still like to know what happened last night."

"You were talking in your sleep for one thing," Tree replied, ducking the fact that he and Freddie had gotten Twist drunk in the first place.

"Yeah? What was I saying?" Twist's eyes had narrowed even further.

"You were shouting something that sounded like monster…and begging forgiveness."

"That's bullshit." Twist's battered face darkened. His eyes blazed. "You're trying to gaslight me."

"No, I'm not," Tree protested.

"I knew this was a bad idea. I never should have agreed to this. To hell with you." Twist spat the words out. "You get too close. You push too far. Accusing me of shit. Go to hell—and stay away from me!"

He lurched out of the car, slamming the door hard.

20

Rex was in the office when Tree got there, working away at the keyboard of his computer. There was no sign of Gladys. Rex glanced up at Tree. "Long time no see," Rex said. He went back to attacking his keyboard.

"What are you working on?" Tree asked, seating himself at his desk.

"Volume two of my memoirs," Rex said in a way that suggested everyone should know that. "My esteemed producer thinks we may get another season out of Netflix. I don't know where he gets that idea, but he wants to be prepared."

"That's good news," Tree said.

"As long as that bastard John Twist isn't involved the next time."

Tree decided it was best not to add fuel to the angry fire burning inside Rex by mentioning where Twist had spent the night. "Have you seen Gladys?"

"Not in, as you can see. She's never in. I don't know what's wrong with her—don't know what we're paying her for."

"Her argument might be that we're not paying her enough, given how her job description has, shall we say, broadened," Tree said.

Rex kept hitting his keyboard. "You broadened it, not me."

No arguing that, Tree thought. Tree watched his friend for a time, debating whether to make the phone call he was considering.

He decided to take a wild chance and dialed the number he knew far too well. It rang for so long, Tree was beginning to think that Cee Jay Boone of the Sanibel Police Department wasn't going to answer. "What the hell do you want, Tree?" Cee Jay demanded unhappily when she finally answered.

"It could be that I'm calling simply to see how you're doing," Tree said in his best innocent-caller voice.

"You mean it's been a while since you've been in trouble," amended Cee Jay.

"Oh, I've been in lots of trouble, it just hasn't involved the police."

"Yet," added Cee Jay.

"Tell me something," Tree said, grabbing the opening he hoped she had left for him. "If I was to give you a license number, do you suppose you could check it out for me?"

"There, I knew it," Cee Jay declared, satisfied that her suspicion about the call was correct.

"Could you do that for me?" Tree pressed.

"Now why would I do anything for you?"

"If this was a movie, I'd say something like, 'because you owe me one.'"

"This isn't a movie, and I sure as hell don't owe you anything. In fact, I'd say it's you who owe me about ten."

"Can you make it eleven? For old time's sake?"

"There is no 'old time's sake.' If I thought about what had happened dealing with you in the so-called old times, I would hang up."

"For future consideration, then."

"Jesus, Tree. This is beyond the pale, even for you." She paused. "What kind of future consideration are you talking about?"

"Future consideration to be determined." Limp, Tree thought, but all he could come up with on short notice.

"All right," Cee Jay said in exasperation. "You've worn me down—as usual. Give me the number."

"It's a vanity plate. LENNY1."

"Why? Why do you want this number?"

"That's part of the future consideration I'm talking about."

"I'll get back to you." She clicked off.

Tree closed his phone and refocused on Rex. He wasn't so much typing as angrily striking blows. His mouth was hard set. He seemed lost in a silent fury. Tree rose and went over, drawing a chair up to Rex's desk and plunking himself down. Rex continued to strike at the keyboard.

"Don't bother me," he snapped. "I'm very busy—as you can see."

"Yes, I can see that you are," Tree agreed quietly. "Are you all right?"

"Why does everyone always ask that?" Rex slowed his typing so he could rant. "Every goddamn movie you see, people are constantly asking each other if they're all right. It's a senseless question that only gets asked when you're not all right at all."

"You're not all right—right?" Tree ventured.

Rex finally stopped hammering at the keyboard. He looked exhausted from his efforts. "I don't know what I was expecting with this goddamn movie," he offered sorrowfully. "Some sort of satisfaction, I guess. Celebrating a life lived, I don't know. *Something.* Instead, I'm feeling like shit. I wish I'd never written that book—which is full of lies, in case you didn't know."

"No, I didn't," Tree said, taken aback by Rex's assertion. "You mean you didn't sleep with Joan Crawford?"

"That part's true," Rex said. "In fact, I slept with her twice."

"There you go then," Tree said.

"I was a whole lot happier before I wrote that book," Rex said morosely. "Not the way it's supposed to be."

"You shouldn't let Twist get to you," Tree said.

Rex gave him a fierce look. "It's not Twist, goddamnit!"

"Then what is it?"

"I don't know what it is… it's everything. It's not what I thought it would be."

"I suppose it never is," Tree said.

"I want it to be, I want it to be more…somehow. Always did I guess." Rex became unexpectedly reflective. "When I first got to Hollywood, I saw myself as this square-jawed hero on the screen, sweeping beautiful women into my arms as the cameras rolled and everyone looked on in awe of my movie-star charisma. Nothing like that ever happened. I discovered that I wasn't going to be discovered, that I wasn't a movie star. I was no better than any of the hundreds of other young men with the same dreams, having their hopes dashed just like me."

Tree didn't know what to say. You have the fantasy, he thought. There's always the fantasy—and then it gets destroyed by reality.

At his desk, Tree's cellphone started ringing. "I'd better take that," Tree said.

"Yeah, you'd better," Rex said. He got to his feet at the same time Tree did.

"Where are you going?" Tree asked.

"Out. What difference does it make?"

"I'm worried about you, that's all."

"Don't worry about me. I'm going to be famous, remember?"

"I forgot for a moment," Tree said.

"Yeah, well, it's going to happen anytime now. So don't go too far away."

"No, I won't," Tree said. His phone continued to ring.

"I've got a couple of errands to run," Rex said. "I'll be back."

He started for the door and then stopped. "Twist was right," he said.

"About what?"

"I blew the line. Simple goddamn line. 'You're under arrest, pal,' and I couldn't get it out. I wasn't a movie star. I wasn't even an actor."

He went out the door.

Tree picked up his cell as Rex disappeared. He shouldn't have this feeling, he thought guiltily, but he was actually relieved that Rex had left. Tree didn't know how to deal with his old friend when he was like this. The production was a mess, no question, as movie productions usually were, and Twist was turning out to be a complication no one expected. But he would soon be gone, and then Rex hopefully could relax and enjoy his newfound fame, as fleeting as it might be. They would all be able to relax, Tree thought as he opened his cell.

"Have you seen Twist?" Holbrook sounded panicked.

"I dropped him off at the Lighthouse Restaurant an hour ago," Tree said.

"He's not here. Everyone's going crazy."

"I'm on my way," Tree said.

21

Tree closed the phone and turned to see someone coming into the office. A muscular, dark-haired young man in tight, faded jeans and a blazing white T-shirt that showed off his pecs. With a start, Tree recognized the young man from the Cotton Blossom who was tased by Gladys.

"Hey, how you doin'?" The young man confronted Tree, taking a threatening stance, hands in fists on either side of his slim hips.

"I'm doing fine, but I'm in a hurry," Tree said. "What can I do for you?"

"What you can do for me, man? No, you got that wrong. It's what *I* can do for you."

"And what's that?"

The young man was looking around, moving restlessly. "What is this place, anyway? They're selling fish bait out there." He eyed Tree with a smirk. "You sell bait, do you?"

"Like you said, it's available in the other room," Tree said quietly.

"You're supposed to be some sort of private eye, right?"

"That's right. Why don't you tell me what I can do for you?"

"Yeah, okay." The young man exhaled a breath. "Okay, here's what I can do. I can make sure I don't go to the press with my story about how this famous asshole John Twist assaulted me after I turned down his sexual advances. What do you think about that? You think that will help you and your movie-star pal—who I never heard of incidentally, but I hear he's real big in Hollywood."

"What's your name?" Tree demanded.

"You can call me, Diego, how's that, Mr. Tree Callister?" He grinned. A nasty grin, Tree thought. "That's right, I know your name, man. How do you like that?"

"What do you want ...Diego?"

"Hey, it's Florida, right? What does everyone in Florida want?"

"Let me guess," Tree said. "Money."

Diego's face lit up. "Bingo, man! You got that exactly right. Moola. Greenbacks—that way, I keep my mouth shut."

"First of all," Tree said, working to keep his voice level, anxious to be rid of this guy and get out of there, "I don't have any money. And I doubt Mr. Twist has any either. Secondly, you and your pal assaulted Twist. Not the other way around."

Tree could see Diego's expression turning hostile. "Right now," he continued, "I don't have time for your blackmail bullshit so step out my way."

"You're making a big mistake." Diego raised those fists as if to demonstrate how big a mistake Tree was making.

"I doubt it," Tree said. Although watching Diego, he was beginning to wonder about that.

"Let me give you a little taste of what's gonna happen..."

Before Tree could do anything, Diego delivered a hard blow to his shoulder that knocked him back against his desk. Tree fought to stay on his feet as Diego lunged for him. "You don't talk to me like that, man. You show me respect. You don't diss me."

"Get out of here," Tree managed to gasp.

"Get out the greenbacks, man. Then we talk about future plans, you know? Ways to keep me happy so I keep my mouth shut."

"Hey—dickhead," called a voice behind Diego.

He swung around to find Gladys poised in the doorway. The angry arrogance fell away, replaced by a flicker of fear, quickly hidden by a nasty smile. "There you are, lady. I was hoping I'd run into you again. Get me a little payback."

"I believe you've been asked to leave. Do as you're told. Get out."

"I don't think so." Tree wasn't quite sure where it came from, but all of a sudden, the long blade of a switchblade knife gleamed in Diego's hand.

"Don't you get it, you sorry jerk," Glady said. "When you bring a knife to the party, make sure someone else doesn't bring a gun."

That's when Gladys made sure he could see the SIG Sauer she held.

The gun brought Diego to a stop. He looked a lot more nervous. He tried on an uncertain smile. "You're not gonna shoot me, lady."

"Are you kidding?" sneered Gladys. "Where do you think you live? This is America, pal. You show up here, young kid threatening with a knife, and I shoot you, the state gives me an award. Make a move and you won't be on television tomorrow, but I will be, a local hero, standing my ground."

Diego looked more uncertain. He lowered the knife. "I'm gonna go to WINK TV, man. They'll eat up my story."

"Then you'd better get going," Gladys said.

She kept her gun trained on Diego as she moved away from the doorway in order to let him pass. "You'll be sorry." Diego didn't sound very convincing.

"I'm already sorry," Gladys said. "But an asshole like you has nothing to do with it."

Diego went out the door. Tree exhaled, releasing the tension he had been holding in. "Jesus," he said.

"More evidence that I shouldn't let you out of my sight," Gladys said, shoving the gun back into her shoulder bag.

"Thank you—yet again," Tree said.

"Like I always say, it beats answering the phone," Gladys said.

"Where have you been?"

She dropped her shoulder bag on her desk. "You're not going to believe this, but I've been with John Twist."

"You're kidding," Tree said, astonished.

"He phoned me in my truck," Gladys explained. "He said he wanted to meet. He said he'd been feeling guilty all these years over what he did to me, and wanted to make amends. In a moment of weakness, I agreed to see him."

"Where was he? Everyone's looking for him. He's supposed to be on set."

"He's at his house. At least he was when I met him."

"What happened."

Gladys's face darkened. "The same shit as before. No big surprise, I suppose. Once an abusive monster, always a monster."

"Tell me what happened," Tree urged.

"When I got there, it was evident he had been drinking. For a time, it was okay. He said how much he had cared for me, but then he went on, denying he beat the shit out of me. I reminded him that he was a scumbag and a liar, and that's when it started to get nasty."

"How nasty?" Tree felt the tension rising in him once again.

"Put it this way, unlike how it was when I was a kid named Blue Streak, this time the reupholstered Gladys Demchuk came to the party with a gun."

"You didn't use the gun by any chance?" Tree was holding his breath.

"He's all right," Gladys said. "Gave him a scare, that's all. But I should never have gone around there."

"I'm sorry, Gladys."

"Don't be sorry. You had nothing to do with this."

"This probably explains why he hasn't shown up on set. I'd better go around and see if I can get him there so we can get him the hell out of our lives."

"Be careful, Tree," she said. "He can fool you. No matter what you want to think, the monster is still a monster. Believe me, I know."

———————

As soon as he was off the causeway turning onto Periwinkle Way, Tree called Clay Holbrook. "Has he shown up?" Tree asked as soon as the producer answered.

"No, he hasn't," answered Holbrook angrily. "We're all ready to kill him. One more goddamn day and he pulls this shit."

"I know where he is," Tree said. "I'm on my way to pick him up."

"Please hurry, we're dying here."

No vehicles were in the driveway when Tree got to Twist's rented house. As he parked, he wondered how Twist had gotten here from the Lighthouse. Why did he leave so soon after Tree dropped him off? Because Gladys agreed to see him? He would find out shortly, he told himself as he came up the steps to the front door. To his surprise, he found it ajar. It looked as though Gladys had left in a hurry, not bothering to close the door behind her.

Tree pushed it a bit more and called, "John? It's Tree Callister. Can I come in?"

There was no answer. Tree's heart sank. Had he already passed out? What was he going to do then? And even if he could bring him around, would Twist be in any shape to film? He stepped inside, immediately sensing something was wrong. "John? Are you here?"

He had started across the living room when he saw Twist lying on the carpeted floor between the coffee table and a sofa. There was a bottle of Scotch on the table. Two tumblers were beside the bottle, one empty the other half full.

Tree's worst fear, a dead-drunk immobile movie star. He thought about calling Holbrook, but then decided to try to wake Twist and see if he couldn't get him going.

He bent over, saw the bullet hole in Twist's chest, the blood-soaked shirtfront, and knew that there would be no moving John Twist ever again.

22

Tree had witnessed this scene far too many times: the needless convoys of police, fire and emergency vehicles arriving far too late, the revolving flashing of multicolored lights, the platoons of police officers in crisp uniforms representing various regional law enforcement agencies, everyone standing around in groups, speaking intently—about what? Tree wondered.

John Twist was dead. There was nothing anyone could do about that, except stand around and talk about it. They might solve his murder. Bring the killer to justice. But most of those present were not going to do that. It was up to the detectives who had now arrived on the scene, Cee Jay Boone and Owen Markfield.

When he had first encountered Cee Jay fifteen years ago, she had tried to kill him. Cee Jay denied it, of course. Over the years their relationship had evolved to the point where Tree was more or less certain she no longer had his murder on her mind.

Most of the time.

The original slim young woman who had made his life miserable had aged into a plump, middle-aged investigator who made his life miserable. The short dark Afro of her youth had become a short gray Afro. Tree liked to think they had developed a grudging admiration for each other, although as she approached him this late afternoon, she didn't look particularly admiring. Exasperated was probably a better description of the expression on her still-handsome face.

Owen Markfield was a different matter entirely, Tree reflected. He hadn't ever tried to kill Tree—although he gave every indication he'd like to do it on occasion—but he had never developed an admiration, grudging or otherwise. Hatred was a better word for how the detective felt.

When Tree first met him, Markfield would have made a great television cop. He looked the part with his blond-tipped perfectly cut hair, his perfect square jaw, his perfect blue eyes. A perfectly tanned, Southwest Florida Robert Redford back in the day. But now Redford had disappeared into a pudgy guy with thinning blond hair, no longer camera-ready for network TV. All these years later though, Markfield still maintained the same fierce disdain that originated the first time he threatened to throw Tree in jail for the rest of his life. Tree had not yet been thrown in jail, which hadn't stopped Markfield from eagerly issuing the threats.

Like now…

"Let me get this straight," he said, his voice filled with familiar disbelief, "they hired *you* to protect John Twist?"

"To keep an eye on him, yes," said Tree.

"Well, you haven't done much of a goddamn job, have you?"

"Okay, let's take it down a notch," Cee Jay said, playing her role as the soul of police professionalism.

"At least he's not accusing me of the murder for a change," Tree put in.

"Yet," added Markfield.

"Tell us what happened, Tree," Cee Jay said.

"It's like I told the officers when they arrived," Tree began, "I dropped Twist off at the Lighthouse at about 10:30 this morning."

"He'd spent the night at your house, is that right?" asked Cee Jay.

"He'd been drinking at his house." Better not to say who had induced that drinking. "My wife and I thought he should stay with us. That way I could be sure to get him to the set on time in the morning."

"All right, so you dropped him off at the Lighthouse..."

"Then I went back to the office, did some work for the next couple of hours." Omitting the would-be blackmailer named Diego who showed up with a switchblade.

"Anyone else with you?"

"Rex was there, but he soon left." Never mind Gladys with the gun against Diego's knife, Tree thought. Unnecessary detail that would implicate Gladys. Right now, for her own good, he didn't want her drawn in.

"Go on."

"That's when Clay Holbrook, Twist's producer, called in a panic to say that his star had not appeared. I came around here a little after noon and found him dead in the living room. I then called the police."

"All very neat," Markfield said with something approaching disgust. "Your story wrapped up in a tidy bow. Now let's dig in and get to how many lies you've told."

Quite a number of lies, actually, Tree thought. In his dedication to being eternally suspicious of what Tree told him, Markfield ended up being disconcertingly accurate.

Of course, Tree was not about to admit that.

"What makes you think I'm lying?" Tree added an edge to his voice, as though any accusation of deceitfulness could only induce incredulity. Besides, he wasn't actually lying, simply omitting a few facts that would only complicate matters.

Like maybe Gladys had shot Twist in a fit of anger.

"All you ever tell us is lies," Markfield insisted.

"Let's suppose for a change you're telling us the truth," Cee

Jay interjected. "You've been around John Twist for the past few days. Am I right about that?"

"Yes, that's correct," Tree said.

"Do you have any idea who might have wanted to kill him?"

Who would want to kill, John Twist? There were any number of candidates, Tree thought. Where to start. If he was being honest, then he would have to put Gladys at the top of the list. She had just been with Twist and she had a gun. But he didn't want to start with her. He didn't want her mixed up in this. Not yet. Knifing-wielding, blackmailing Diego could be another candidate. He might have left Tree's office in a fury, gone to Twist's house, confronted a drunk, belligerent actor and ended up shooting him. Then—and they would be close to the top of the list—Shell Dean and Mr. Dix could have found out where Twist lived, gone around and shot him. A very real possibility. He could safely talk about those two, and there was the added benefit that he might actually be identifying the culprits.

"Shortly after Twist arrived on Sanibel, I was visited by two men," Tree explained. "One of the men was Shell Dean. Shell said he owned casinos in Reno, Nevada. He claimed John Twist had abducted his fiancée, a woman named April May."

"His fiancée was called April May?" Markfield's voice dripped with disbelief.

"That's what Shell told me. He believed that April was with Twist. He wanted me to find her."

"And did you?" Cee Jay asked.

Answering that question meant Tree would have to step away from the comparative safety of a few omitted facts and start outright lying—doing exactly what Markfield always accused him of doing. "No," he announced. Then he headed back for something that was more or less true: "April certainly wasn't with Twist at the house. He was alone as far as I could see."

"You said there were two men." Cee Jay was scribbling in her notebook.

"There was his associate, a Mr. Dix."

Cee Jay glanced up from her notebook. "Does he have a first name?"

Tree shook his head. "Mr. Dix was all I got. Although Shell described him as an associate, he came across as Shell's personal bodyguard, someone who did the dirty work when it needed to be done."

"Like killing a movie star who might have run off with his boss's woman," Cee Jay suggested.

"You would have to say it's a possibility," agreed Tree.

"Casino operators named Shell. Kidnapped fiancées. Body-guards without first names," piped up Markfield in disgust. "Here we go again. It's all Tree Callister bullshit."

Cee Jay gave Tree a sharp look. "Is that what it is? Bullshit?"

"All I'm saying is that if you're looking for suspects, which I'm sure you are, you should look at those guys. They have a motive, and Dix sure gives you the impression he is capable of doing something like this."

"Do you know where we can find these people?" Cee Jay asked.

"I don't know," Tree said.

"These two hired you and you don't know where they're staying?" Markfield said in disbelief.

"They gave me a card with a number on it," Tree said.

Markfield was shaking his head as Cee Jay asked, "You'll get me that number, right Tree?"

"Sure," Tree said agreeably.

"Do you expect to hear from them again?"

"I don't know," Tree said. "If they killed Twist, probably not."

"If they do, try to find out where they are," Cee Jay said. "Can you do that for us?"

"You know I'm always happy to cooperate with law enforcement," Tree said.

Markfield jabbed an angry finger in Tree's direction. "Don't think you're getting away with this shit, Callister. We've got a dead goddamn movie star here and who shows up but our favorite Sanibel Island murder suspect. You better believe you haven't heard the last of this."

"I believe anything you tell me, Detective Markfield. You know just how much respect I have for you."

Markfield lunged forward, eyes on fire, raising a fist. Cee Jay stepped in front of him. "That's enough." She spoke with authority. "Mr. Callister knows what buttons to push with you, Detective. Don't let him do it."

"Son of a bitch," growled Markfield. He was taking deep breaths, lowering his fist.

Cee Jay turned to Tree. "Get the hell out of here, before I run you in myself."

23

Tree was in his car when the enormity of what had happened sank in. John Twist was dead. Correction: John Twist had been murdered. Rex's dream was shattered. What's more, there was the strong possibility that Gladys Demchuk soon would become the prime suspect in Twist's murder. Not to forget his own role. Failing to inform the police that Gladys had been with Twist just before he died. An accessory? With Markfield breathing down his neck, why not?

Trouble. Big trouble.

He thought about calling Gladys and then immediately decided against it. Too easy to trace any telephone calls to her. Too easy to trace the phone calls he made to anyone at this point. His cellphone rang. It was Freddie. No harm in talking to Freddie.

"God, Tree, I just heard on the radio," reported a distraught Freddie.

"I found him when I went around to the house," Tree said. "I just finished with the police. They've been jumping all over me."

"I feel sick. Where are you?"

"In the car. Not feeling great myself. I'm on the way to the office. I'm concerned that Rex hasn't heard yet."

"Come home soon, please." There was a pleading note in her voice. Unusual for Freddie, Tree thought. He felt a pang of sadness.

"Yes, I want to be with you," he said. "Let me have a word with Rex and then I'll be along."

"Give him a hug for me," Freddie said. "This is all so terrible…"

To his surprise, when he got back to the office, Tree found Clay Holbrook with Rex. They did not look happy to see him.

"I guess you've heard," Tree said as he joined them.

"I came over to give Rex the news," Holbrook said. He looked pale and tired.

"Bastard," Rex said, his voice in a low, angry register. "He does everything he can to screw up the movie and then he goes and gets himself killed."

"I'm sorry, Rex," Tree said. The words sounded hollow. "So sorry."

"You must have found him when you went around to check his house," Holbrook said. He wasn't looking at Tree when he said it.

"That's right," Tree said. "Someone had shot him. I've been with the police until now."

"I would ask you if there are any suspects, but that's a stupid question, isn't it?" Holbrook said. "Where John is concerned, there is no end to the possible suspects." He paused and then added, "You could even add me to the list."

"Me, too," said Rex.

"And what about you, Tree?" asked Holbrook pointedly. "Can we cast you as a suspect, too?"

"I don't think we should be talking like this with the police around," Tree cautioned.

"Why is that, Tree?" Holbrook's voice had turned cold. "Maybe because you're more of a suspect than you'd like to think. After all, you were supposed to protect John, weren't you? It looks like you failed badly. So perhaps you're as responsible for John's death as his killer."

The accusation left Tree speechless. "Let's not get carried

away." Rex's tone was unexpectedly conciliatory. "It's been a bad day. We're all on edge. Let's not start accusing each other of shit we don't mean."

"I'm not saying anything I don't mean," Holbrook snapped. He was on his feet. "I'll be in touch, Rex, as soon as I figure out next steps, although right now I have no idea what those steps might be."

"I've got an idea," Tree said.

The two of them looked at him with equal expressions of disinterest.

"Rex," Tree said.

"What about Rex?" Holbrook demanded.

"Rex can play Rex."

They both looked at him blankly.

"Who better to play the character of Rex Baxter than the actor Rex Baxter?"

"I'm not an actor," Rex protested gruffly.

"Yes, you are. You underestimate yourself. You always have."

Rex made an uncomfortable face but said nothing.

"Twist is gone and that is tragic. But you need a replacement, Clay, and you need him fast. Otherwise, the whole project is dead. Am I right?"

"Yes," Holbrook admitted tightly.

"Here is your replacement, right in front of you."

Holbrook, actually adjusted his glasses to peer at Rex as though seeing him for the first time. "Let me think about it," he said brusquely. He looked pointedly at Rex and repeated, "I'll be in touch."

He turned and marched out without another word.

"You're crazy," Rex said to Tree.

"I've had crazier ideas," Tree responded.

"Offhand, I can't think of any," Rex said.

"Listen, Twist was no shakes as an actor," Tree pressed. "You can do a better job because you already know the character—what's more, you care about him. Also, you don't have nearly as big a gut."

"But Twist was a star, and I'm not."

"Hardly anyone under the age of seventy even remembers John Twist—although that could change now. This will make you the star you've always wanted to be."

"Go to hell," Rex said.

"Incidentally, thanks for coming to my defense with Holbrook," Tree said.

"He's pretty shaken up," said Rex.

"I know, but he's not totally wrong, either," Tree conceded. "I didn't kill Twist, obviously, but I was supposed to protect him, and I didn't."

"Don't make yourself out to be any more important than you are," Rex replied sternly. "You were supposed to try to keep the bastard sober and make sure he got to the set. No one said anything about keeping the killers away."

Tree placed his hand on his old friend's shoulder. "Are you going to be all right?"

"There's that, 'are you all right?' question again. Yes, sure. As long as you can the movie star talk with Holbrook."

"I put the suggestion out there and he didn't jump up and down protesting. We'll see. The next move is up to him."

"He's probably going to shut the whole thing down," Rex said morosely.

"He's got another option on the table."

"If I start to feel sorry for myself, all I have to do is think of Twist. I hated the bastard, but I sure as hell didn't want him to end up like this." He looked up at Tree. "Have you heard from Gladys?"

"Not a thing," Tree said, fearing that since the news of Twist's murder broke, she had gone to ground for a second time.

Or she was on the run.

"I've tried her cell a few times, but she's not answering—as usual. I wonder if she even knows."

Tree silently wondered too. "Call me if you hear from her. Meanwhile, I'd better get home. Freddie's pretty upset."

"Sure, get out of here. Go home and hold your wife."

"Why don't you come with me?" Tree said.

"The two of us holding Freddie? That may be taking friend-ship too far," Rex said with a faint smile. "In answer to your oft-asked 'are you all right?' question, I will be fine. I just need some time alone. Now go."

"Holbrook will be in touch," said Tree confidently. "It's too good an idea to ignore."

"Go to hell," Rex repeated. Not so gruff this time.

"I've been on my way for some time now," Tree said.

"We'll get there together," Rex said.

24

When Tree got home, he did exactly as Rex suggested, he held Freddie. Freddie gripped him fiercely, as though all the bad things—murder included—could be pushed away if they held onto each other.

Except they couldn't.

"What's wrong?" Freddie asked, pulling away from him slightly.

"I'm worried about Gladys," Tree said. "I haven't been able to get hold of her."

Freddie twisted a bit so that she could a better look at her husband. "Why do I have this sinking feeling that there is something you are not telling me—maybe a lot of somethings?"

"There is the one thing," Tree conceded.

"Uh, oh," Freddie said.

"Gladys was with Twist earlier this afternoon."

Freddie reacted with a mixture of surprise and concern. "I thought she wasn't going to have anything to do with him."

"I thought so, too—but she went around to see him."

"How do you know this?"

"She told me that's where she had been when she came back to the office."

"If she killed him, why would she come back to the office and tell you she was with him?"

"Trying to establish an alibi, maybe. It didn't go well with Twist from what she told me. He was drinking, denied beating her years ago. It got pretty ugly, according to Gladys. She ended up pulling a gun on him."

"You don't think—"

"I don't know," Tree answered. "I would like to think that she didn't—didn't pull the trigger. She said that's as far as it went. But somebody shot him."

"Is Gladys capable of doing something like that?"

"In the heat of the moment? Gladys? Yeah, I suppose it's possible. When there is a gun around, anything is possible."

"Oh, God," Freddie groaned, and buried her head against his shoulder.

Tree's phone rang. He removed himself from Freddie's embrace to look at the screen. It was Cee Jay Boone.

"Tell me that Leonard James Foyle of Cape Coral, Florida, has nothing to do with John Twist's murder," Cee Jay said.

"I don't know who that is," answered Tree.

"It's the name registered to LENNY1, the license number you gave me."

"That's another case," Tree said quickly. Which, in all probability, that was true, he thought.

"You're sure?" Cee Jay didn't sound convinced.

"Do you have an address?" Tree asked.

"You're not answering me, Tree." Her frustration with Tree, always just beneath the surface, was bubbling up.

"Yes, it's something else," Tree said, wishing he was a better liar—or perhaps wishing he hadn't become such a deft liar.

She gave him the Cape Coral address and then: "Where's Gladys Demchuk?" That came out of the blue, catching him off guard.

"Why would you ask me that?" Tree answered, playing for time. Suspecting this was the real reason Cee Jay had called.

"Just answer the question, Tree." Cee Jay said impatiently. "I give you something. Now you give me something back. Where's Gladys?"

"I have no idea," Tree answered—truthfully this time.

"If she gets in touch, tell her it's important she calls me, do you understand?"

"Sure," Tree said noncommittally.

"Tree, if you're lying to me, so help me—"

"I'll try to get in touch with her," Tree interrupted. "You have my number."

Cee Jay hung up.

"That didn't sound good," Freddie observed.

"No, it didn't."

"The fact that they already appear to have Gladys in their sights—not helped by the fact that they can't get hold of her."

They were no longer holding one another. They traded fearful looks.

"What's this about a license number?" Freddie asked.

"It's probably nothing," Tree answered. True, but not quite truthful, either. "Something I was asked to follow up, that's all."

That's all, he thought. Right now, though, he had a lot more to be concerned about.

25

"My arms are killing me," Tree heard himself saying, beseechingly. Hardly surprising, he surmised, seeing as how he was still tethered to the bicycle seat high up on the rough timber that was the cross of Calvary, his arms outstretched so that he could get his hands into the false hands attached to the crossbeam.

"You're in pain," Cecil B. DeMille hollered through a megaphone. "You're Christ, you are suffering for all mankind."

"But I'm not Christ," Tree called down. "I'm not supposed to be here."

DeMille, positioned at the foot of the cross, shook his head in disgust. "Don't be such a baby." His voice, amplified through the megaphone, brought chuckles from members of the film crew scattered around the cross.

"You said it was a long shot," Tree moaned. "You said that's all you needed."

DeMille was motioning for a crew member to bring back the ladder. He positioned it near the cross. He handed the megaphone to one of his assistants and then clambered up close to Tree. His bald head gleamed in the reflected light of the big kliegs.

"You don't seem to understand." DeMille was speaking quietly, commandingly, into Tree's ear. "This movie, the piece of film magic in which you have been blessed to play a small but important part, will change cinema as we know it. This movie is groundbreaking. It will be remembered forever. You, young man, are a part of *motion picture history*."

"Mr. DeMille, I hate to tell you this, but it won't be long before no one even remembers your movie. It will be totally forgotten in the rush to produce talking pictures."

"*Talking...pictures?*" DeMille's stentorian tone filled with incredulity. "You must be joking. Sound is a passing fad. It won't last."

"It gets even worse," Tree continued, "in the twenty-first century, movies in theatres will become pretty much a thing of the past. People will watch movies on big home screens. It will all be changed yet again. Nothing will be the same."

DeMille, scowling, jerked his head away. His eyes grew wide with alarm. He called down to the assistant lingering at the bottom of the cross. "Bob, get this young man down, and do it quickly."

"Something wrong, Mr. DeMille?" The assistant looked worried.

"This so-called Jesuit priest they have sent us is demented. He fantasizes that he's some sort of oracle sent by our Lord to prophesize the end of movies at the very moment we are creating greatness in movies. Get him down. Get him out of here."

DeMille disappeared back down to the ground. Two ladders were propped against the cross. Workers in peaked caps, their sleeves rolled up to their elbows, incongruously wearing neckties, scrabbled up and went to work loosening Tree's hands. They struggled to pull them out of the fake hands.

"Can't get his hands free, Mr. DeMille," one of the workers announced.

"Get him down from there, goddamnit!" cried DeMille.

Tree's arms hurt even more. He shouted out in pain as the workers yanked at his hands. The bicycle seat on which he was perched came loose and dropped to the ground, leaving Tree dangling from the cross, held up by his imprisoned hands.

He screamed in agony, twisting on the cross. DeMille was shouting something he couldn't make out. The pain grew worse. He couldn't get loose. The workers on either side of him cursed and continued to yank vainly at his hands.

Finally, the yanking and pulling was too much and the fake hands ripped away from the cross. With an agonizing scream, Tree plummeted to the floor, landing with a loud thump. "Get up!" DeMille bleated, leaning over him, his face red and enraged. Tree managed to get to his knees. An old man walked past, dressed only in a loincloth. "Rex," Tree cried out.

Rex looked down at Tree, but didn't say anything.

"What are you doing, Rex? Why are you here?"

He came to a halt, regarding Tree with a beatific smile. "Mr. DeMille has been kind enough to cast me as Our Lord in his magnificent production. Mr. DeMille will make me a star."

"What?" Tree couldn't believe it.

"I have been cast as Our Lord to help Mr. DeMille tell the greatest story ever told in the greatest film ever made," Rex explained in a gentle tone Tree had never before heard from him.

"Are you out of your mind, Rex? You can't be Jesus!"

"But I *am* Jesus," Rex replied serenely.

"You're too old to play Jesus."

Rex looked affronted. "Don't tell me who I can or can't play. I am an *actor*! I can play *anyone*!"

"No, you, can't!"

"I forgive you, Tree. You don't know what you're doing…"

"That's not the point," Tree shrieked. "They're going to put you on a bicycle seat and then put your hands in fake hands! Don't do it, Rex! Don't!"

Tree continued screaming as he jerked awake. The cross was gone. So was DeMille. And Rex. He was alone in his own bedroom. His arms hurt. Freddie came into the bedroom holding his cellphone. "You were yelling and screaming again," she stated.

"I was back at Calvary," Tree reported. "I fell off the cross. They were replacing me with Rex to play Jesus."

"What are you talking about?" Freddie looked baffled.

"I tried to tell him that he's too old, not to do it. He wasn't listening."

This time Freddie merely grimaced before handing him the phone. "Speak of the devil. It's your man, Jesus, down from the cross and calling you."

Tree took the phone from Freddie. "Rex?"

"They want me to audition." The words came out in a panicky burst.

"It's the role you were born to play," Tree said.

"I can't do it," Rex cried. "I'm no actor. Twist was right. I never was. I can't act."

"Yes, you can," Tree said insistently. "When is this supposed to happen?"

"This afternoon, but I'm gonna phone and cancel."

"Don't do that, Rex. Where is the audition?"

"They want to do a scene they originally shot with Twist at Bowman's Beach. This time with me in it."

"Where are you now?"

"I'm at the office—shivering."

"I'm coming around to pick you up," Tree said. "I'll take you there. It'll be fine."

"No, it won't!" Rex exclaimed.

26

The sky over Bowman's Beach was threatening. There were news reports of a gathering storm aimed at Southwest Florida, but after all it was hurricane season and there were always reports. Besides, thought Tree as he turned down the road toward the beach, hurricanes were the least of his concerns.

This time there was no big crane and only about a quarter of the crew that had been present when Twist filmed there. But there was a camera, and Tak Shindo in his cargo shorts was busily hopping around checking last minute details in preparation for the shoot—just like on a real movie.

"All set?" asked Clay Holbrook, coming to meet them as they stepped off the path leading from the parking lot. From what Tree could see, it was a new Holbrook greeting them this morning. Rested and refreshed and apparently ready to embrace his newest leading man as he shook Rex's hand. "How are you feeling?"

"Nervous," Rex replied promptly.

"You'll do fine," said Holbrook reassuringly. "I have to tell you, everyone I talked to is very excited about this, particularly Tak."

"Glad one of us thinks so," Rex said, gloomily.

A gnome-like man in a baseball cap approached. "Morning all," he said merrily.

"Here's Teddy now. He's our very able first assistant director. "Teddy is going to take you over to makeup. How's that?"

"Sure," said Rex. He looked more nervous than ever as he went off with Teddy.

As soon as they were out of sight, Holbrook turned on Tree, his previously sunny mood evaporating.

"This had better work." He jabbed a finger at Tree for emphasis.

"He's a whole lot better than he thinks he is," Tree said.

"I hope so," said Holbrook shortly.

Rex emerged from the makeup trailer thirty minutes later. By now, the wind had picked up. The sky had darkened more. Rex didn't seem to notice. Tree watched him follow the first assistant director across the beach to where Tak waited behind the camera that had been set up close to the shore. Rex still looked like Rex, but better somehow, Tree thought. It could be the makeup, but there was something else, a different aura around him. The way he walked had changed too. It was more authoritative. Watching him come to a stop beside Tak, Tree understood suddenly what he was witnessing, even before a camera rolled, the birth of a movie star. A movie star of a certain age, yes, but definitely a movie star.

"We've gotta move fast, we're about to lose the weather," Tak said to Rex. "Are you ready to try a take?"

"Ready as I'll ever be."

The scene required Rex to repeat what Twist had shot. A walk across the sand to the water's edge, and then peer reflectively off to the horizon, lost in thought, remembering a long-ago life. This time, though, there was no fancy crane shot, just the camera following Rex. "All right, everybody," called Teddy. "Settle please."

Rex returned to what was his first position at the head of the path into the parking lot. Tak Shindo called, "Action." Rex started his walk. There was something majestic about that walk, Tree thought as he watched his old friend. Not unlike Twist's, but different—better. More human. The walk of a man moving toward his past, proud, yet at the same time fearful. That combination of strength and fear was reflected on Rex's face. Rex wasn't acting Rex Baxter. He *was* Rex Baxter.

He reached the beach. The wind whipped around him. He stopped, stared out into what looked like the coming storm swirling around a life lived. He paused for a couple of beats as the camera moved in on him. Then he turned, faced the camera and said, "You're under arrest, pal."

"Okay, cut!" Tak charged out from behind the camera, his small face bright with excitement. "Terrific!" He pronounced enthusiastically. "Just what I've always wanted but haven't been able to get until now." He paused, looking confused. "But what was that last bit all about?"

"Nothing," Tree heard Rex say. "Something I had to get off my chest, that's all."

Tree and Holbrook traded knowing glances.

Tak hurried over. "This is the guy!" he announced happily. "He's everything Rex Baxter should be!"

"He *is* Rex Baxter," Tree pointed out.

"Why didn't we have this guy from the beginning?" demanded Tak.

"Netflix wanted a star," Holbrook said.

"Well now we've got the right guy," Shindo said with a big grin. "This guy's gonna be a star!"

Tree gazed at Rex, still on the shore, not moving, trying to control his emotions, Tree suspected. He couldn't be sure, but he could have sworn he saw a tear roll down Rex's cheek.

————

"How do you feel?" Tree asked as he drove Rex home. It had begun to rain, a soft steady tropical downpour.

"Alive," Rex said, slumped beside him, seemingly exhausted. "Like I haven't felt alive for a long time."

"You really nailed it," Tree said. "I didn't know if you could pull it off—I *hoped* you could do it, but I didn't know. But you did, you pulled it off magnificently."

"It felt good," Rex allowed. "I know that what's happening—might happen—is the result of a tragedy, but you know what? I don't care. It felt really, really good."

"Just enjoy it," advised Tree. "An hour ago, you didn't think you could do it. Now you know you can."

"No small thanks to you," Rex said.

"I had nothing to do with it," Tree said. "All I did was drive you."

"Without that drive, without you behind the wheel, I never would have done it," Rex said. "I owe you one."

"You don't owe me anything," Tree said as he came to a stop in front of Rex's house.

"You know, I love you," Rex said.

"I love you too." Tree gripped Rex's hand hard.

Rex opened his mouth to respond, but his voice choked. He took his hand away and got out of the car. Tree watched him disappear into the rain.

27

John Twist's murder topped the local news cycle. The murder pushed the political craziness of the day out of the lead position on the cable news networks. Reporters and camera people from the various news organizations were soon pouring onto the island. Everyone wanted to talk to Rex. They had not yet discovered where he lived, but they soon staked out the Cattle Dock Bait Company.

Even though Tree had discovered Twist's body, the police, thankfully, had not released that information. Thus far he had been spared press scrutiny. Despite what everyone felt was a brilliant screen test by Rex, Clay Holbrook had not been in touch and had kept the production shut down. There was worrisome speculation that Netflix, in the wake of John Twist's murder, could scrap the production entirely. After all, they had lost their star, with a week left to shoot.

Gladys's whereabouts continued to be unknown. At a brief press conference, Cee Jay Boone announced that police were seeking Gladys Louise Demchuk—Tree had no idea her middle name was Louise—as "a person of interest," a sure sign in Tree's estimation, that she was high on their list of suspects.

No mention, Tree noted, was made of Shell Dean or Mr. Dix. They too seemed to have disappeared.

Tree felt helpless, not sure what to do next, uncertain about Gladys and the part she might have played in Twist's death. Unsure of anything, except the uncertainty of everything. What's more, he was haunted by his reoccurring dream—hanging on a cross while Cecil B. DeMille berated him for even suggesting silent movies didn't have much of a future. What was that all about?

"Don't ask me," Freddie advised. "I've had to put up with any number of your weird dreams over the years. I would say they usually have some relevance to whatever trouble you find yourself in at the time."

"I prefer to call them the cases I was investigating," Tree amended.

"The trouble you found yourself in," Freddie reiterated. "The cases you stumbled through."

"You're being very harsh," Tree complained.

"I'm trying to help you explain your dreams. The more trouble you're in, the more that you worry, the crazier your dreams. Cue you on a cross with Cecil B. DeMille."

"Actually, DeMille isn't on the cross. It's only me. In a loincloth."

"I stand corrected," Freddie said. "I must say, though, you may be one of the only people in the world who has dreams about Cecil B. DeMille. Knowing that, we can ascertain the depth of your craziness and understand just how much trouble you are in."

"Sounds very scientific," Tree suggested.

"It is, and only an experienced professional such as myself knows how to apply the science."

"This may explain how it is possible for you to stay married to me."

"It's a challenge, let me tell you." Freddie smiled when she said this—to Tree's relief.

"Okay, you've analyzed my bad dreams, I put a stop to them by—"

"Getting yourself out of the jam you're in," Freddie declared.

Easier said than done, Tree thought. So much easier said, than done…

"There is something." Freddie's voice interrupted his reverie.

"What's that?"

"The license number you were after…"

"LENNY1."

"Whatever happened about that?"

"To my amazement, Cee Jay actually came through for me. The vehicle is registered to a guy named Leonard Foyle, but I don't know that has much to do with anything."

"Doesn't it?" Freddie raised an eyebrow.

"Big Lenny, as his wife calls him."

"Okay, Big Lenny," Freddie said. "Where does Big Lenny live?"

"In Cape Coral."

"Where he has his boat," Freddie added. "Might be worth a drive out to Cape Coral."

"I guess," said Tree dubiously. "Although I don't see the point."

"No harm in driving out there," Freddie suggested. "At least it will give you something to do. Take your mind off things so that you don't wake up thinking you're nailed to a cross."

Yes, Tree thought. It might at least do that.

———

Tree had just reached Cape Coral when Rex called. He sounded morose. "I got a call from Clay Holbrook."

"To say you've got the part," Tree said hopefully.

"They all like my so-called screen test, everyone was very impressed…"

Tree's heart sank. He slowed his car. "Do I hear a but…?"

"Netflix has decided that despite everything that's happened, they want to go ahead and finish the production."

"That's good news, right?"

"Good news except that in order to do that, they feel they need a star. Holbrook tells me that Harrison Ford has agreed to take the role."

"You're kidding." Tree couldn't believe it.

"He's flying in next week. Clay wants me to meet with him."

"Rex, what can I say? I'm so sorry."

"Hey, welcome to Hollywood."

Tree turned into the marina. "Where are you now?"

"Where do you think? At the office. Holbrook insists he's interested in a sequel, particularly now that they've got Ford."

"I'm out at Cape Coral, but as soon as I'm finished here, I'll come around."

"No hurry. I don't want you to worry about me," Rex said. "I'm a big boy. I'll be fine."

He cut the call off.

Tree sat for a time feeling numb and, once again, helpless against the unseen forces that work to deprive guys like Rex of any kind of a break. Him too. While he was feeling sorry for Rex, he might as well feel sorry for himself—the missed opportunities, the failures, a lifetime of rejection. He and Rex had taken the blows together, believing—fantasizing—that somehow, someday, things would be better. But things didn't get any better. Or if they did, it was momentary. They'd give it to Rex, then promptly take it away again. Anger welled up inside him, but anger was useless, a waste of time. There was nothing Rex could do. There was nothing he could do.

He exhaled loudly and got out of the car, blinking against the harsh light, reminded that he had forgotten his sunglasses.

The ranks of pleasure craft at peaceful rest shone brightly under the unrelenting noonday sun. Tree was perspiring before he got to the part of the dock where *Archer* was supposed to be anchored. Only it wasn't.

Instead, the *Black Marlin*, which Tree imagined was deep underwater in in the Gulf of Mexico, sat majestically in its berth. Tree could hardly believe what he was seeing. But then Tree was having trouble believing anything these days even when he saw it.

There was, however, the thought-stopping reality of the snout of the gun pressed against his ribs. The gun made him forget about Rex. The gun made him stop feeling sorry for himself. The gun scared him. He had a moment to reflect all over again that he was too old for this, too old for guns in his ribs. But then this was Florida and Mr. Dix didn't appear to have any qualms about age. He probably didn't care if Tree was too old. He was old enough to be shot, that was for sure. And Mr. Dix, as Tree had suspected from get-go, was just the man for the shooting.

"Why don't we hop aboard?" Mr. Dix had a way of making the invitation sound ominous. The gun helped. So did the shove forward Dix gave Tree.

They climbed the teak steps to the deck, Mr. Dix keeping the gun where Tree could see it. Shell Dean, a doughy potentate in white, was sprawled on a deck chair. A potentate wearing dark glasses and, incongruously, a captain's peaked cap. He managed a smile when he saw Tree with Mr. Dix. "This is an unexpected surprise," he said, not particularly happily, Tree noted.

"But not a pleasant one," said Mr. Dix, maintaining his position behind Tree.

"Oh, I don't know about that," said Shell easily. "We were

bound to run into our friend sooner or later. After all, we did pay you three thousand dollars, didn't we, Tree? You certainly wouldn't let us down. You being an honorable man."

"Last thing I want, Shell, is to disappoint you," Tree replied. "I'd be glad to give you a refund."

"No, no." Shell waved a hand around, as if to swat away the idea. "If you look at it from a certain perspective, you did your job. You found John Twist for us. I could fault you, I suppose, for keeping certain facts from us."

"Like the fact that he was right under your nose and you lied to us," grumbled Mr. Dix. Tree noticed he hadn't stopped pointing the gun at him.

"Yes, there is that, Mr. Dix," Shell agreed. "You hire a detective and he immediately starts lying to you. But there you go, and really, now, it's a moot point. Don't you agree, Mr. Dix?"

"Not necessarily," said Mr. Dix darkly.

"I mean, Twist is dead, isn't he? Tree, did you kill him? You certainly had the opportunity."

Tree shook his head. "No, I didn't. But then, I could ask you and Mr. Dix the same question, couldn't I? In fact, unless I miss my guess, it's the same question the police would like to ask. Only they are having trouble getting hold of you."

Shell waved that thought away with another flutter of his hand. "Even though we had ample reason to murder the bastard, Mr. Dix and I must plead not guilty. Whoever killed Twist probably also killed my fiancée, and the man who apparently was Twist's stand-in or stunt double."

"You know the police are looking for you," Tree said.

"Which is why we thought it best to take a cruise for a while, until things cool down."

"Things haven't cooled down," Tree said.

"We understand that," Shell said. "This is where you come in."

"Bad idea," Mr. Dix interjected. He had yet to put his gun away. Not a good sign, Tree thought.

"Be that as it may, Mr. Dix, we don't have a lot of choice." Shell eased himself out of the deck chair to address Tree. "We need you to find John Twist's killer. Mr. Dix doesn't think you can do it."

"Isn't that something the police should be doing?"

"Our concern is that the police could be fixated on the two of us and won't be spending a lot of time looking for anyone else. You know we're innocent, therefore you can concentrate on finding the real killer."

Tree addressed Shell. "I don't think you should be relying on me."

"I hate to say you're our best hope," he said in a resigned voice, "but I'm afraid that's what you are."

"Not exactly a ringing endorsement," grumbled Mr. Dix.

"If neither of you murdered Twist, then who might have?" Tree asked. "Any ideas?"

Mr. Dix traded looks with Shell. He shrugged. "Frankly, I thought it was only me and Mr. Dix who wanted the bastard dead."

"Not much to go on," Tree said.

"Nothing to go on," Mr. Dix said.

"The best thing would be to make yourself available to the police," Tree said. "You'll look a lot less guilty if you talk to them."

"They're just as likely to lock us up," Shell said. "Right now, I don't want that. For the time being Mr. Dix and I are contemplating a Mexican cruise. What do you think, Mr. Dix?"

"I don't like Mexico," said Mr. Dix, gruffly. "Country's full of narcos."

"For the moment, Mexico is the safer bet," Shell said. He turned to Tree. "What do you need from me, Tree? A retainer?"

"No, it's fine," Tree said. "The three thousand is enough."

"More than enough," echoed Mr. Dix. Tree noticed that his gun had disappeared. A step in the right direction.

"You sure this is what you want?" Tree said to Shell.

"I don't think there's a lot of choice," he answered.

"Okay," he said. "I hope you know what you're doing."

"I wouldn't go that far," Shell said with a smile that was unexpectedly winsome. "Find us a killer and everything will be all right."

Yes, he thought, that's all I have to do. But how?

28

Tree no sooner drove away from the marina than he began having his typical second thoughts—third and fourth thoughts, when it came down to it. He assured himself that he hadn't really agreed to anything, but even so, what he had become involved in could make him complicit in Twist's murder. The two said they were innocent. But were they? They had the motives necessary to kill Twist. And now he was becoming part of it.

What's more, he wasn't even sure where he was driving. How had he ended up in front of the address in Cape Coral where Big Lenny and his wife resided? That wasn't too much of a mystery. He had the address after all. But what did they have to do with anything? This then was a waste of time, something to do while he figured out how to extract himself from the latest jam he had gotten himself into.

More questions. More doubts.

The rambling ranch-style house sloped down to a man-made lake. He drove to the park at the end of the street where he positioned the car so that he had a view of the house. Like most of the neighborhoods throughout Florida, no one seemed to occupy the nearby houses. Where did everyone go? he marveled yet again. To their pleasure craft? Couldn't be. No one ever seemed to take their boats out, either. Florida was the empty state. People said they were here, but they weren't.

Leonard James Foyle and his wife appeared to be among the absent. The Range Rover he had seen at the marina with the LENNY1 vanity plate wasn't in the driveway.

What was the point of even sitting here? He hated stakeouts. He was terrible at them. He thought of phoning Freddie and then quickly dismissed that idea. He didn't want any record on his cellphone of where he had been, and he certainly shouldn't give out any unnecessary information about his encounter with Shell and Mr. Dix on the *Black Marlin*.

Down the street, a Range Rover flashed into view. Tree sat up, watching as the vehicle turned into the driveway. LENNY1 had arrived home. Actually, it was the wife of LENNY1 who got out of the vehicle. She wore the regulation Florida uniform consisting of shorts and a T-shirt. Tree had to admit that from this distance, LENNY1's wife, as she had on the *Archer*, looked pretty darned good. She opened the rear door and lifted out grocery bags and then, lugging the bags, went into the house. The neighborhood returned to its customary stillness.

Brought on by age and boredom, Tree started to do what he always tended to do during a stakeout, what no self-respecting private eye should. He began to doze off. Jerking his head back up, forcing himself to focus each time he nodded off. He was shaking himself awake for the umpteenth time when LENNY1's wife reappeared. She had changed into a short skirt that emphasized the shape of her legs. She appeared to have added makeup and had done something with her hair. Tree was wide awake, watching as she got behind the wheel of her Range Rover.

Tree waited until she was headed down the street before he started after her.

He followed her across the Cape Coral Bridge onto Daniels Parkway, keeping his distance as she turned south on I-75. Traffic was heavy as she drew close to Naples. She swung onto the Golden Gate Parkway and then Tamiami Trail. Reaching Third Avenue, she parked in a lot behind the street. Tree watched while she handed a boyish attendant her key fob. Deciding it was too risky to leave his car in the lot, he left the Mercedes on a nearby street. He crossed the parking lot and came out onto Third Avenue in time to spot LENNY1's wife entering the terrace of an Italian restaurant.

Tree walked along to the restaurant partially hidden from the street by a wall of sweet-smelling bougainvillea. Through the bougainvillea, Tree could see that the terrace was crowded with lunching patrons. At a table near the rear of the terrace, a tall, striking black man in a navy jacket held a chair so that LENNY1's wife could be seated. The black man took a seat across from her. He reached across to take her hand in his. She looked at him fondly, or so it seemed to Tree from his vantage point on the sidewalk. Whoever this guy was, he definitely was not LENNY1. When their waiter arrived with menus, the black man reluctantly removed his hand. The waiter smiled and nodded as the black man indicated LENNY1's wife. He appeared to be ordering drinks for the two of them.

The crowds thronging Third Avenue made him feel self-conscious, aware of being an old guy standing there ogling the well-to-do luncheon patrons. Okay, maybe not *that* old, but certainly standing out— imagining he stood out. He was about to move on when someone grabbed his arm. "Easy does it there, chummy," a voice said.

The hand on his arm belonged to a balding man in a tan sports jacket and an open-collar blue shirt. A second man with a head of short-cropped hair moved against him. He wore an linen shirt, untucked. The balding man's grip tightened on Tree's arm. "Let's move you along," he said with quiet authority.

"What is this? What's going on?" Tree managed, over his shock at being accosted.

The balding man responded by tightening his grip, sending bolts of pain shooting through Tree's arm.

The guy with the crew cut flipped open a billfold to reveal a Federal Bureau of Investigation identity card with a gold FBI badge beside it. "We need you to come with us," the agent with the crew cut said.

"Why? What have I done?"

A black Ford SUV had drawn up at the curb. The guy with the crew cut put away his ID and went over and opened the passenger side rear door. The balding guy with the strong grip guided Tree to the SUV. "Watch your head," the agent advised as he pushed Tree forward into the SUV.

An African-American guy in a white T-shirt was behind the wheel as the other two agents crowded in. The balding man with the grip sat in front. Crew cut sat next to Tree. The guy in the white T-shirt eased the SUV forward into the traffic.

"Let me ask you this, chummy, are you armed?" This came from the balding agent, twisting around so that he faced Tree.

"Does it look like I'm armed?"

"I don't know, chummy. That's why I'm asking you."

"No," Tree said. "I'm not armed."

"Chummy, why don't you show me some ID?"

"You mean you don't know who I am?" Thinking, why would you pick me up off the street?

"Sure we do," replied the balding man. "You're the asshole I'm asking for some identification."

"I'm going to pull my wallet out of my back pocket." In case they suspected he might go for the gun he said he didn't have.

"Sure, chummy, why don't you do that?"

Tree extracted his billfold and showed them his private detective's license.

The balding man studied the license intently as though it might contain hidden clues. He glanced up at Tree with a smirk. "What do you know? A private dick. W. Tremain Callister?"

"That's what the license says," Tree said.

"Address on Captiva Island? That's current, is it?"

"It is," confirmed Tree.

"W. Tremain… What does the W stand for?"

Tree hesitated and then gritted his teeth before he said, "Wilbur."

That drew another smirk out of the balding man. "Well, Wilbur, you're a bit far afield here in Naples, aren't you?"

"No, I come to Naples all the time," Tree said. "Why sometimes, I go as far as Miami."

"But what specifically brings you to Naples today, Wilbur?"

"I was about to have lunch at that restaurant," Tree replied smoothly. Perhaps he wasn't such a bad liar after all, particularly when it came to members of the law enforcement community.

The balding man didn't look convinced. "Here's what we're going to do, Wilbur, since you're lying to federal agents. We're going to take you in for further questioning."

"I'm not lying to you," Tree lied.

"Wilbur," I want you to hold your hands out for the agent beside you."

"Why do you want me to do that?"

"Because I'm telling you to."

Tree thought he'd better comply. As soon as he held out his hands, crew cut guy snapped handcuffs on his wrists."

Then, before he could object, crew cut guy dropped a black hood over Tree's head.

The world disappeared.

29

During the short ride that ensued, no one said anything. Tree found that a hood over his head got in the way of casual conversation. Besides, before he could think of anything to say, the SUV came to a stop. Hands pulled him free of the interior. He was promptly hustled forward. He heard a door opening and sensed that they had guided him into a building. Industrial cleaning odors assailed his nostrils. Another door opened and he was pushed through it. He was guided a few more yards before being eased onto a chair. He heard a door close. Silence followed. Tree sat there.

And sat there.

Okay, he knew this drill. The suspect was left alone to stew in his own juices, giving him time to wallow in his growing fear of what was about to happen to him, and decide he'd better confess all to his interrogators. Except, what was he supposed to confess to the FBI? He had been standing on the street, minding his own business, for God's sake. Of course, there were all sorts of things he *could* confess if pressed. But how would the FBI know that?

Okay, he had to concede, more or less minding his own business.

His reverie was interrupted by the sound of a door opening and footsteps making their entrance. A moment later, the hood was yanked off his head.

Tree blinked into a light that obscured a clear view of the reed-thin woman who now confronted him in an all-too-familiar white-walled interrogation room. This particular room lacked the usual two-way mirror and there were no cameras that Tree could see. The thin woman would be in her late forties, Tree guessed. The high cheekbones, the long angular nose, the thin lips set in a permanent grimace reminded him of Miss Haight, his eighth-grade teacher. She used to hit him with a wooden ruler. Tree doubted he would get off as lightly this afternoon.

The thin woman wore a dark-blue business suit, the epitome of authoritarian professionalism. She leaned back against a metal table, the only other piece of furniture. She leaned with her arms folded, appearing to study him, much like a specimen under glass she didn't particularly like the look of.

"Are you going to beat me with a rubber hose?" Tree asked finally.

"I'm hoping that won't be necessary, but if it comes down to it, yeah, sure, a rubber hose is an option."

"I guess I'd better hope that's not what it comes down to," Tree said.

"Yeah, Mr. W. Tremain Callister, you'd better hope that's case." She unfolded her arms and straightened up. "I'd better introduce myself. I'm Special Agent Jane Nugent, and I'm here to inform you you're in a shitload of trouble."

"Since I haven't done anything, Special Agent Nugent, I don't see how that's possible," Tree said, adopting what he hoped was an expression of confused innocence—the everyman who was the victim of mistaken identity.

"You see W. Tremain, you are now on my radar screen and that's not a good thing at all," Special Agent Nugent went on, apparently oblivious to Tree's earnestly adopted innocence. "The FBI I represent is not your typical FBI. I'm the badass FBI, the off-the-books FBI. The we-don't-give-a-shit-what-we-have-to-do-to-get-the-job-done FBI."

"Okay, that's good to know," Tree said, mustering as poised

a manner as he could manage, "but I still haven't done anything wrong. And you still don't have any right to hold me."

"We don't huh? Let me ask you what you were doing tailing Susan Tyler?"

Susan Tyler? Tree thought. So that was the name of LENNY1's wife. At least he had learned that much. Small satisfaction as they threw him into prison and tossed away the key.

"It's part of an ongoing case I'm involved in," Tree explained. A lame answer, he had to admit, that never convinced anyone in authority. But there was a certain amount of truth to it in this instance.

"What kind of case are you talking about?"

"I'm not at liberty to say." Which was true. Kind of true.

"You're not?" Special Agent Nugent raised dismayed eyebrows. "Let me fill you in on what you, a dipshit amateur, have stumbled into and nearly managed to screw up. You have thrown into jeopardy an undercover FBI operation that has been over a year in the making. Now, thanks to you, our prime target suspects something is amiss—something she did not suspect before you happened along."

"Obviously, I had no idea," Tree said, trying to wrap his head around what the agent was telling him.

"I wonder about that," said Special Agent Nugent. She moved away, refolding her arms, as though a more distant view of him might help her ascertain his threat level.

"You wonder?"

"If you might not be working with Susan Tyler."

This was getting crazier by the minute, Tree thought. Out loud, he said, "You're probably not going to believe this, but until now, I didn't even know the woman's name."

"Then what the hell do you think you're doing following her?" It was the FBI agent's turn to look mystified.

"I've asked that question myself many times, over the years. But in this particular instance, as I told you earlier, I was hired to keep an eye on her."

"I ask you again. Who hired you?"

"Same answer, Special Agent. I'm not at liberty to say."

"You're a screwup, W. Tremain Callister." She paused as though pondering what to say next. "However, the fact that you're such a stumbling fool could turn out to be a good thing for us."

"How exactly do you make the stumbling fools of the world a good thing for you?" Tree asked, fearing what was to come next.

"Thanks to your fumbling attempts to follow her, Susan Tyler has become suspicious that she is under surveillance. As a result, we are concerned that she might go to ground. But if you let her know you're the one who is watching her, for reasons that have nothing to do with a federal investigation, then there is a good chance she will lower her guard again."

"I know I'm an amateur and everything," Tree offered, "but that sounds like a really dumb idea."

"Maybe so," Special Agent Nugent said agreeably, "but it's *my* dumb idea, therefore you're going to make it happen."

"And what happens if I don't?"

"Then the handcuffs stay on and we dump you down a dark hole until you decide to come around."

"You can't do that," Tree said, not very confidently.

"You bet I can," Agent Nugent said with a lot more confidence. "I can do anything with you I want. I'm not your typical FBI, remember?"

"Thanks for reminding me," said Tree. "What am I supposed to tell this woman?"

"Tell her why you're following her."

"I don't want to tell her that."

"You're such a fool," Special Agent Nugent said with a shake of her head. "You have no idea who she is, do you?"

"Why don't you fill me in?" Tree countered.

"Ten years ago, Susan was a Hollywood starlet, acting under the name Susie Stevens," Special Agent Nugent explained. "Then she ended up in hospital badly beaten. She told police at the time that she had been assaulted by a famous actor she had been seeing. She refused to reveal his name so police couldn't press charges. From what we know, Susan left Los Angeles shortly after she recovered and moved to Florida. That's when she became Susan Tyler again, met and married Leonard Foyle—Big Lenny as everyone calls him—and embarked on a carefree life of crime. Which we are now doing our best to bring to an end—with your help."

"What kind of crime are we talking about?" asked Tree.

"That guy she was having lunch with?"

"What about him?"

"That's Carlos Chacal." She said the name with a certain amount of drama, as though she was revealing a piece of important evidence. The name meant nothing to Tree.

"I should know who Carlos Chacal is, right?" Tree hazarded.

Special Agent Nugent rolled her eyes in exasperation. "Yeah, you should. If you want illegal drugs in Southwest, Florida, as far north as Sarasota, as far south as Miami, Carlos Chacal makes sure you're well supplied. By the by, he is also is a ruthless killer. Even the Mexican cartels keep him at arm's length."

"How does Susan Tyler fit into this?"

"Susan and Carlos are having an affair. He is also financing her husband's fleet management business—Fleet Lenny."

"Does Big Lenny know that his wife is having an affair?"

"Shortly after Lenny and Susan married, Lenny's father

died, leaving him the fleet car business. Susan and Lenny took it over and promptly screwed it up. Fleet Lenny was close to bankruptcy. Lenny apparently wasn't a much better businessman. Three years ago, he met Carlos and since then the business has done gangbusters."

"Which is to say what?"

"We think Lenny knows what he needs to know," Nugent said.

"What does that mean?"

"We believe Fleet Lenny's cars and trucks transport drugs north from Fort Myers. That's basically the business Fleet Lenny is in now. The legit part is just a front." She stopped to give him a hard look. "You're the hotshot private detective following Susan. Doesn't any of this ring a bell with you?"

"Maybe I'm not such a hotshot," Tree said.

"No kidding," said Special Agent Nugent dryly.

"Based on my one encounter with him, I would say Big Lenny is the jealous type. I'm not so sure he would like the idea of his wife sleeping with another guy, even if they are in business together."

"Lenny may not have much choice," Nugent said. "Still, if what you say is true, then the way to convince Susan you're following her, is to go through Lenny."

"I don't see how any of this is going to convince either Lenny or Susan of anything," Tree said.

"Let's pretend that you're a smart guy, okay? Tough private detective? You'd better figure it out—and do it fast. We don't have a lot of time." She went over to the table and picked up the hood that was lying there.

"How do I get in touch with you?"

"That's all right, W. Tremain Callister, I'll get in touch with you." She shot a watery smile in his direction. "We know where you live."

She paused holding the hood as though demonstrating a product. "Incidentally, you probably know this, but if you say anything to anyone about our conversation, it will not go well for you."

"What do you think will happen to me?" Tree asked.

"We would probably kill you," Agent Nugent replied, as though killing him was a given.

Then she shoved the hood onto his head and pulled it down.

Once again, his world went dark.

30

Tree was dropped off on Third Avenue at the same spot where they had picked him up. The balding agent pulled his hood off. Crew cut guy freed him from the handcuffs.

"Take it easy there," Wilbur," the balding agent said in a friendly voice, as though they'd just had a drink together. He reached over and opened the door. No one else in the SUV said anything. As soon as Tree was out, the vehicle sped off. Nearby, the staff at the Italian restaurant was setting up for the dinner crowd. Susan Tyler and the apparently notorious Carlos Chacal had long since departed.

Crossing the parking lot behind the restaurant, he saw that the Range Rover was gone. Hardly surprising, he thought as he got into his car. Now what? He started the engine. He had no idea what to do next. Shell Dean and Mr. Dix demanded he find a killer. FBI Special Agent Nugent threatened endless horrors if he didn't make Susan Tyler believe he was following her and not the feds. Every time he made a move, it backfired and he ended up in deeper trouble than before.

The traffic moving north on Tamiami Trail was heavy. His cellphone sounded. Freddie was calling him. What was he supposed to tell her? He couldn't tell her anything without getting her into the same mess he was in. The phone kept ringing. It seemed to go on forever. He didn't answer, feeling, not for the first time in their marriage, like a shit who was betraying Freddie. And he was. Finally, the ringing stopped. He would explain everything, he told himself, when the time was right. Whenever that was. Right now, he did not have a clue.

With the traffic, it took him over an hour to reach the outskirts of Fort Myers. By now, in addition to being fed up with himself, he was growing tired. He wanted to go home, but that would mean facing questions that he couldn't answer. Which would mean more lies—lies piled on lies. The lies would lead to recriminations, and possibly more of the bad dreams that had him nailed to a cross, the price paid for all his multitude of shortcomings.

So many shortcomings…

He drove back to Cape Coral. Susan Tyler and her husband Lenny were in Cape Coral. He had vague notions of knocking on their door and announcing, "I'm following you. Don't pay any attention to those *other* people who you might suspect are following you. They're not following you. I am the one following you. Just don't ask me *why* I am following you. I'm not sure about that."

It was dusk by the time he reached the house. As before, it didn't look as though anyone was home. The Range Rover was not in the driveway. He wasn't certain whether to be disappointed or relieved. He parked on the street and got out, debating whether to simply march up to the front door and knock. What the hell? he thought. Why not?

He came along a stone walkway winding to the front door. He pressed the doorbell. From inside he could hear the sound of electronic chimes. No one responded. He pressed the bell again. Nothing. He tried the latch. The door swung open. He pushed at it so that he could call out, "Hello?"

There was no answer. He stepped inside to a vestibule that opened on a wide, slightly sunken living room, blandly furnished. He crossed into the kitchen area. There was a refrigerator and stove, but nothing else. A rear door opened to a pool deck and a swimming pool. It took Tree a moment before he saw the dead body floating against the side.

Venturing closer, Tree could make out the pale profile of Leonard James Foyle—LENNY1. The one eye Tree could see bulged sightlessly.

Fight or flight, he thought, standing in the fading sunlight. There was no fight, encountering yet another dead body. Only flight.

Blindly, he circled around the house and back to the street where he had left his car—the car that anyone in the neighborhood looking out a window could plainly see and identify to police: *That's right an older guy driving a Mercedes. Yes, in fact I did take down his license number. There's been so much suspicious activity at that house...*

Shit! he thought.

He walked to the end of the deserted street, certain that the neighbors were watching this suspicious-looking old man who seemed so out of place. He got behind the wheel and started the engine, hoping against hope no one was watching. He drove off along the street.

———

In the omnipresent silence of the marina at night, the wind howling around him and dark threatening clouds hiding the moon, Tree could see that, as he suspected, the *Black Marlin* had departed for parts unknown. But the *Archer* had returned to its berth. He contemplated the fact that here was the start of all his trouble. But that was probably unfair. His trouble started the day he decided to be a private detective on Sanibel, an island where nothing ever happened.

Except something had always managed to happen to him.

But he could change that right now. All he had to do was leave and go home to Freddie, make his confession while nestled in her loving arms. But then what? Wait for the FBI's evil Jane Nugent to arrive with her rubber hose before throwing him into some federal hellhole for the rest of his life? Or how about Shell and Mr. Dix? A matter of time before they showed up, and Dix had a gun that he was only too glad to point in Tree's direction.

Besides, he consoled himself, it didn't look as if anyone was on the craft, anyway. For the moment, he was safe.

For the moment.

He clambered onto the deck, listening to the creak and groan of the vessel, lifted his face to the stiff breeze full of sea scents. He moved over to the hatchway, and then dropped down into the darkened cabin, not sure what he was looking for. Not sure he was looking for anything. But there it was, inviting, left on a shelf above the sofa—a Glock automatic.

The Glock was wedged between tightly wrapped packages the size of bricks. He opened an adjacent cupboard. It too was stuffed with brick-sized packages; cocaine, Tree surmised. He found brick-filled garbage bags in cupboards beneath the counter.

He went back to the Glock and wriggled it out from between the bricks. He pressed the magazine release using his thumb and with his other hand pulled out the clip. It was fully loaded. He shoved the clip back into the gun. Who leaves a loaded handgun lying around? he wondered. But then this was Florida. People left loaded guns everywhere. Particularly people who smuggle shipments of cocaine in their pleasure craft. People who might require a gun at a moment's notice.

He took the Glock back up to the deck and sat with it on the captain's chair in the cockpit. He got his phone out and poked out the number he had been given earlier.

"I wasn't expecting to hear from you so soon," Shell Dean sounded surprised when he came on the line.

"Where are you?" Tree demanded.

"Like I told you before," Shell replied carefully. "On a sea cruise. Why do you ask?"

"I'm onboard the *Archer*," Tree said.

"Ah, yes. The lovely Susan and her thug-like husband. What have they got to do with anything?"

"The boat is jam-packed with packages of cocaine. Do you know anything about that?"

It took a moment or two for Shell to reply. "Why should I know anything about cocaine?"

"I don't know," Tree said. "That's why I'm asking."

"Not a thing," Shell replied. "What are you doing on the *Archer?*"

"Waiting," Tree said.

"Waiting for what?"

"Maybe a killer," Tree said.

———

To his relief, Shell didn't call back as he sat and waited. Despite what he had told him, he had no idea what he was waiting for. He was equally uncertain that the real killers weren't out there somewhere in the Gulf, while he wasted his time here. The Glock in his hand provided him with a modicum of comfort. He was an American with a gun. What could possibly go wrong?

He heard footsteps coming along the dock, the stomach-dropping reminder that plenty could go wrong. In all likelihood, it was just about to go very wrong. He shifted around in the captain's chair, gripping the gun more tightly, so that he was ready as Susan Tyler came on the deck, followed almost immediately by a tall black man he assumed was Carlos Chacal. Briefly, in the darkness, they failed to notice him.

When Susan did see him, she drew in her breath sharply. Chacal, on the other hand, showed no emotion, as though he had plenty of experience with men sitting in the darkness with guns.

He wore a black T-shirt, shorts, and, incongruously for a drug-smuggling killer, Tree thought, flip-flops.

"You're the fellow looking to buy a boat," Susan said calmly. She wore form fitting white jeans and a white blouse. Her hair fell softly to her shoulders. He could easily imagine her on a network television series. She would be perfect casting for the attractive, slightly older woman giving the series star more trouble than he could handle.

"That's me," Tree agreed. "I'm that fellow."

"Did you find a boat?" she asked in a strained voice. Tree noticed Chacal's eyes had become narrow apertures. He could practically hear the machinery turning in his head, searching for the way to gain the upper hand.

"I'm afraid not," Tree said.

"I remember your name," Susan said. "It's something like Oak, isn't it?"

Chacal let loose a bray of laughter. "This dude is called Oak?"

"Tree," Tree corrected. "Tree Callister. And I'm not looking for a boat. I'm looking for the two of you."

Did that sound a whole lot more melodramatic than he intended? Susan and Chacal's smiles appeared to confirm that it did. "Why would some guy I don't even know come looking for me with a gun?" Chacal asked.

"It could have something to do with you killing John Twist," Tree said.

Silence followed, accompanied by slightly confused looks from the couple.

Susan found her voice first. "That's the movie star, right?"

"That's right," Tree acknowledged.

"What makes you think either one of us has anything to do with his death?" Susan now sounded more perplexed than strained.

"Years ago, Twist was out of control drinking and taking drugs. He beat up a young actress he had been dating. He put her in the hospital. What he did to the young woman should have ended his career. But he was able to pay her off. The young actress left town, finished with Hollywood. Disenchanted after what Twist did to her."

"I'm not sure how this has anything to do with me," Susan said.

"I think you are the actress whose career was destroyed by Twist."

"Me?"

"You met Lenny here in Florida, married him, and through him you became friends with Carlos, the killer who could help you accomplish what you had been thinking about ever since you left Hollywood."

"And what's that?" asked Susan.

"Revenge," Tree said, once again trying not to sound too melodramatic. "When you heard Twist was in the area making a movie, that's when you decided to act. At first, I thought it was you and Lenny. But now I believe it's Carlos. With him, you had the services of a professional who could do the job right. You found out where he was living on Sanibel. The initial plan was to kill him there. But then you were sunning yourself on this boat and who should walk past but John Twist himself.

"You watched him go the yacht at the end of the dock and board it. You could hardly believe your luck. You phoned Carlos. He came around. By now it was night, and Twist was still on the yacht. It was a perfect setup. Carlos went to work. He slipped on board. He shot Twist in the face and then, because he wasn't about to leave any witnesses, he shot the woman with Twist. Carlos left the yacht and went back to the *Archer* where you were waiting to cast off the lines and take the *Archer* out to sea with no one the wiser. The perfect getaway."

Tree paused and then added, "Except for one thing."

"I can't wait to hear what that could be," Chacal said. Beside him, Susan's face had become immobile.

"You shot the wrong man. It wasn't Twist. It was Bronco Holiday, his longtime stand-in and stunt man. The guy who did his dirty work for him. The woman was April May. She was engaged to a guy named Shell Dean. Shell was angry that his fiancée was involved with an aging movie star. Twist probably knew he was in trouble and sent Bronco hoping he could negotiate some kind of deal. Shell and his man Mr. Dix must have found the bodies and rather than have to deal with the police, they took the yacht out into the Gulf of Mexico where they disposed of the bodies."

"So then what did we do?" Chacal asked the question more as an interested audience member inquiring about the next part of an engrossing story than someone hearing the details of the murders he'd committed.

"You didn't give up. You waited until the real John Twist was alone at his house, and then came for him. This time you got it right."

In retrospect, Tree should have been more aware of someone who, according to the FBI, was as lethal as Carlos Chacal was. He should not have been so caught up in the telling of his story, ensuring the couple understood just how brilliant a detective he was.

Given his size, Tree could only marvel at the lightning speed with which Chacal moved. He landed a smartly delivered punch that knocked Tree out of the captain's chair. The Glock flew out of his hand. Chacal immediately moved in and slugged Tree in the mouth. He was spitting blood and teeth as he tumbled back, crashing down the staircase, landing hard on the cabin floor with a loud crack of his head.

The burst of intense pain sent him spiraling into a black void.

31

The warm blood trickling down his face brought Tree back to something like consciousness. Not that he wanted back when he realized in darkness he was propped upright in a chair, his arms wrenched behind him, his wrists wrapped tightly in duct tape. His ankles too so that he could hardly move.

There was the high whistle of the wind, the boat's creak and sway. Presently, footsteps sounded coming down to him. Susan Tyler appeared carrying a facecloth. She leaned down to use the damp cloth to clean the blood off his face. "I was raped in Los Angeles, you got that right, and it nearly destroyed me, no question." She spoke quietly, barely above a whisper. "But you're wrong about John Twist. It wasn't him. Someone famous, yes, but not Twist."

She went over to the sink, washed out the cloth and then returned to dab at his face some more. The warmth felt good.

"I saw Twist come along the dock and recognized him, but that was the extent of my involvement with him," Susan continued. "Carlos came by later and we took the boat for a cruise."

"Was that before or after you killed your husband?" Tree asked.

She took the facecloth away to give him a hard look. "You got yourself quite a knock on the head, Tree. It's caused you to think all sorts of crazy things. I would say you should see a doctor, but unfortunately with Carlos here, I don't think that's going to happen."

"What is going to happen?"

"We're headed out into the Gulf," she said, standing up. "Nothing good happens out there."

She dropped the now-bloody cloth onto the nearby counter. "I'll do my best for you," she said in a voice that made it sound as if there was not a lot of hope her best would be good enough.

That didn't sound good, Tree reflected. Not good at all.

———

He had lost consciousness again. When he came around, his mouth was full of blood. He ran his tongue around, feeling the spaces where a couple of his teeth had been. He spat out a wad of blood as Carlos Chacal came down the stairs holding the Glock he had taken away from Tree. He seemed to fill the cramped space of the cabin. He wore exactly the kind of expression—a combination of seriousness and determination—Tree would have expected of a killer. A killer who was about to kill.

Chacal lifted the Glock up as though it was a prop for the lecture he was about to deliver. Not much of a lecture. "The only way you could have found this. That means you saw what you shouldn't see. You understand?"

"I didn't see anything," Tree said lamely.

"And the only way you could know about Susan, someone must have told you," Chacal went on. "I suspect it must have been the FBI."

"That's not true," Tree lied weakly.

"Then there is this weird notion you seem to have that I killed this John Twist character—an actor I'd never even heard of, incidentally, before I heard about his death on the news." He paused with what looked to Tree like an expression of sorrow. "As you can see, you're a liability to me, a liability that's come pushing into my life from nowhere, one that won't go away unless—"

He stopped in mid-sentence, his face becoming blank, hearing the churn of an engine growing louder. This was quickly followed by a high-pitched scream from Susan, calling his name.

Chacal sprinted across the cabin to lunge up the stairs as Susan's screams rang out again. There was a volley of gunshots. Susan's final piercing scream rose above the blasts. Then silence. Then a second volley—loud pops echoing above him. The thump of something—or someone—hitting the deck. Then more silence.

An ominous silence.

After a while, Tree heard movement. Voices, although he couldn't quite understand what they were saying. He struggled in the chair, trying to free himself, discovering he was no threat to the duct tape. He thought of calling out to whoever was moving around on the deck. Maybe that wasn't such a good idea. After a few more minutes, heavy footsteps clomped down the stairs. A shadowy figure appeared, stopped abruptly, met by the sight of Tree tied to a chair.

"Jesus Christ," said Shell Dean. "There you are, Tree. We were just wondering what had happened to you."

"Well, Shell, they tied me up," Tree said dryly, not certain whether to be relieved at Shell's appearance or more frightened than ever. Leaning toward freightened, despite how ridiculous he looked in his peaked captain's cap. Fear trumped ridiculous thanks to the gun in Shell's hand. He wore a black tracksuit, which had the effect of adding to the scariness.

"I can see that," Shell said.

"You could untie me," Tree suggested.

That gave Shell pause. He nodded and said, "Yeah, I could."

He made no move to actually do it. Which Tree did not find reassuring.

Then Mr. Dix came down the stairs. He too was dressed in a black tracksuit. Instead of a Glock, he carried what appeared to be a lethal-looking semi-automatic AR-15. He too stopped when he saw Tree. Except he didn't say anything, just darted a glance at Shell.

"What do you say, Mr. Dix?" asked Shell. He kept his eyes trained on Tree.

"Well, I'll be," answered Mr. Dix. Tree couldn't be sure in the shadows, but it looked as though Mr. Dix now had trained his weapon in Tree's direction. Not exactly making him feel any more confident.

"What did you do with Susan Tyler and Carlos Chacal?" Tree asked.

"What do you think we did with the two people who you, yourself, informed me killed April and Bronco," Shell said.

"I never actually said they were the killers," Tree said.

"You certainly intimated as such," Shell retorted indignantly. "It was after I heard that from you, Mr. Dix and I decided to come looking for the *Archer*. And sure enough, here we are."

"You shouldn't have opened fire on them," Tree said.

"We decided it was best not to take any chances," Shell said. He turned to Mr. Dix. "What do you think, Mr. Dix? About taking chances?"

"Best not to take them."

"They didn't kill April," Tree said. "They didn't kill John Twist either, for that matter."

"Yes, they did." Shell's tone suggested he was in no mood for an argument.

"They said they didn't."

"Of course, they did. Right, Mr. Dix?"

"What else would they say?" replied Mr. Dix.

"They wouldn't say anything else, would they?" agreed Shell.

"The question now," said Mr. Dix.

"The question?" asked Shell. "What question are you talking about, Mr. Dix?"

"The question of what we do with this guy." He waved the muzzle of his weapon in Tree's direction.

"You could untie me," Tree offered a second time, a little more hopefully.

"I don't think we should do that," said Mr. Dix.

"What do you think we should do, Mr. Dix?" asked Shell.

"I think we should kill him," Dix said unequivocally.

A cold shiver ran down the length of Tree's spine.

32

"He knows too much, he's seen too much—and besides, I don't like him," Mr. Dix stated in a matter-of-fact tone.

Shell appeared to take Mr. Dix's observation under serious consideration. "I don't know about that," Shell said finally. "If we killed everyone you don't like, Mr. Dix, there would be no one left to visit my casinos."

"There are other factors, as I outlined previously," Mr. Dix replied sullenly.

"All things considered, Tree's been pretty good to us. We wouldn't be here having finished the job we started out to do if it wasn't for him."

"We've got a couple of dead bodies up on the deck," Mr. Dix said reasonably. "We let him go, he goes to the cops."

Shell focused on Tree. "He's got a point don't you think, Tree?"

"I'm afraid, he does," Tree said. "Even if I don't go to the police, they won't go away." Not much of a reason for keeping him alive, he thought.

He added: "That guy up on the deck. His name is Carlos Chacal. He's Southwest Florida's top drug lord. He goes missing, a lot of people are going to start asking a lot of questions. And then if I disappear, that only adds to the numbers of police launching investigations."

Shell glanced at Mr. Dix. "Solid argument, Mr. Dix. Solid."

"Desperate plea of a condemned man," countered Mr. Dix. "Nobody gives a shit about dead gangsters—or stupid private detectives."

Well, thought Tree, Mr. Dix was probably right about the stupid private detectives.

Shell gazed at Tree like an undertaker deciding on the size of the coffin. Then he looked at Dix. "Mr. Dix, let's get this man untied and get him up on the deck."

Tree was suddenly having trouble breathing. "What are you planning to do, Shell?" The words came out in a strangled rush of air.

"Mr. Dix is gonna get you untied for starters."

Not at all reassuring, Tree thought.

Shell kept his gaze on Tree as Mr. Dix set his weapon aside to move in on Tree. His face showed no emotion. Except, Tree noted, there was a rigid set to his mouth, as though he was gritting his teeth. A killer gritted his teeth like that, Tree thought. Dix held up a knife and then flicked open its blade. He knelt to cut at the tape binding Tree's ankles. Then he went to work on his wrists. Having cut Tree free, Dix quickly retrieved his weapon and held it steadily on Tree. A necessary precaution when confronting a dangerous hombre like Tree Callister, he thought.

"Come on up on the deck, Tree," Shell ordered. "But let's do it slow and easy as they used to say in the westerns of my youth."

Shell backed up the stairs as Tree followed him. Mr. Dix brought up the rear. Tree, his legs still weak from being bound together, stumbled as he mounted the steps. "Careful there, partner," said Shell.

He cares, thought Tree, grasping for any straw that hinted he wasn't about to get shot and dumped overboard.

On the wind-swept aft deck Susan and her friend Carlos were laid out by the transom. Blood was smeared across the teakwood leading to the bodies, indicating they had been dragged into position. The bigger *Black Marlin* bounced against the side of the *Archer*. Shell and Mr. Dix, two modern-day pirates plundering the high seas, Tree mused. The armed pirates he turned now to confront. Shell looked friendly enough as he eyed Tree. But that could be deceiving, particularly since Dix had his weapon raised and looked all set to shoot him right away and not waste time with the niceties of an execution. That is, if there were niceties around an execution, thought Tree.

Not far from the bodies lay an inflated orange life raft Tree hadn't seen when he came onboard. A pair of oars was fixed to its sides, their yellow blades shining against the uncertain light. Shell saw that Tree's eyes were trained on the raft, and he grinned. "We were thinking of maybe setting your friends over there adrift in it." He nodded at the life raft. "But you can make better use of it."

"You're kidding," said Tree, appalled, unable to take his frightened eyes off the raft.

"No joke," snapped Dix. "If it was me, never mind a life raft, I'd just toss you overboard."

"Now, Mr. Dix," Shell admonished. "We like Tree. He's a good man. Tried his best." He addressed Tree. "Mr. Dix and me, we've got some business that I believe will take care of any evidence that could be helpful to the authorities. Fixing things the way they need to be fixed will keep us occupied for a while prior to setting out on our next voyage."

"Where are you going?"

Shell looked at Dix. "Where are we headed, Mr. Dix?"

"Parts unknown," Dix said.

"There you have it, Tree. Parts unknown. Best you don't know much more than that. After all, you can't talk about what you don't know, right?"

Tree's eyes were still fixed on the life raft. "If I have to get back to the mainland in that thing, I doubt you have to worry about me talking."

"That's the idea," growled Mr. Dix.

"Come on, Tree," Shell said merrily. "A little nautical adventure. Test yourself against the elements. Makes a man out of you."

"I'm man enough as it is," Tree said.

"You could use improvement," muttered Dix.

"You'll be fine," Shell said. "It's not that far to shore. You shouldn't have any trouble."

Sure thing, Tree thought. Navigating Gulf waters amid gale-type winds in the dead of night propelled by what looked like toy oars with plastic paddles. No trouble at all.

"Do you have any idea where we are now?" Tree asked.

"South of Sanibel," Shell answered.

"Head north," advised Mr. Dix gruffly.

———

Tree wasn't afloat in the ridiculously bobbing raft on the roughening Gulf waters for more than ten minutes before his stomach turned and he started feeling seasick. He should not be on water, he told himself, one of the many, many reasons he never should have allowed himself to be talked into moving to Florida. If he survived this, he would gather Freddie and get out of the state. There was too much water. In Chicago, yes, there was one big lake, but staying far away from it was easily accomplished. But now here he was, forever lost in the heaving waters of the Sunshine State, desperate to stay afloat in what was little more than a yellow rubber ducky.

Sharks!

What about sharks? Were there sharks in the Gulf of Mexico? Of course there were. All sorts of them—looking for a nighttime snack. And here it was, easy pickings floating on a rubber ducky.

He refused to think about the man-eating sharks that even now could be circling him. Instead, he occupied himself struggling to work the flimsy oars against the increasingly large swells. He hadn't rowed anything since he was a kid and even then was no good at it on calm lake water in Northern Michigan. He was no good at this stuff, no good at anything except—in his youth anyway—stringing a declarative sentence together. In addition, he was also very good at getting himself into hot water.

Or, in this case, cold Gulf water.

The moon hid behind clouds that had the effect of turning everything around him black; a black sky, a black sea. The bright orange of the life raft stood out against the blackness, as did the flash of the yellow paddles as he dipped them into the black water with no discernable effect. He seemed to be drifting further and further away from the two boats pushed together, their running lights shining out of the blackness. Drifting, but drifting where? His efforts to control the path of the raft were mostly fruitless. He was cold and scared and fearing the worst.

Lost at sea. What an ignominious end, he thought.

The first sign that the world was ending occurred when the black sky disappeared suddenly in a spiraling ball of smoke and red flame rising up off the water. The *Black Marlin's* flybridge ascended spectacularly heavenward, as though being launched into orbit.

A low rumbling followed, increasing in velocity, rolling across the water with such force that it practically knocked Tree out of the raft while at the same time sending it spinning wildly in a suddenly turbulent sea. Tree fought with the oars to keep

the raft upright as the pieces of wreckage that weren't catapult-
ed straight up into the sky, came spinning across the waves toward him. Through thick gray clouds of smoke, he could make
out the two vessels listing badly, burning into the sea.

As he watched, the faint outline of a third craft became visible. A beam of bright light cut through the darkness. It swept
the sea uncertainly for a couple of minutes then settled and
came around to blind Tree slumped at his oars. Maintaining
the light on him, the craft turned and slowed to a stop a hundred yards away. Its wash rocked the raft. Tree gripped its sides,
desperately holding on, his stomach roiling its displeasure.

"Tree Callister," a voice boomed through a loudspeaker.
"Hold where you are. Repeat: hold where you are! Do not
move. We are coming to get you."

In response, Tree leaned over the side of the life raft and
threw up.

33

"The suspects on board one of the boats opened fire as we approached," reported FBI Special Agent Jane Nugent in the formal voice she would probably use when testifying at the official inquiry. "We had no choice but to return fire."

"You blew them out of the water," Tree observed.

"We returned fire," Nugent stated flatly. "My advice to you is not to say anything differently."

They had thrown a blanket around the shivering Tree when they got him onboard and into the cramped cabin of what they told him was a forty-one-foot Coastal Interceptor Vessel on loan from the Coast Guard. There were two others with Nugent, shoulder to shoulder in the tight space, the balding agent and the crew cut guy. The three of them were dressed in windbreakers emblazoned across the back with big yellow FBI letters. At times the up-and-down pitch of the vessel became violent as it lunged across the waves, propelled by a trio of 300-horsepower Mercury outboard engines. Nugent provided him with Dramamine and bottled water so that as he was "debriefed"—their word—his stomach settled somewhat and he began to feel better. Seated close to Tree, Nugent leaned forward, peering at his damaged, bloody mouth.

"What happened to you?"

"Carlos Chacal," Tree said. "He decided to knock some teeth out of my head."

She sat back smiling. "He won't be doing that anymore."

"How did you know where they were?" asked Tree.

"Let's say keeping you under surveillance was a great help

to our investigation," Nugent said. "Thanks to you, we have been able to eliminate one of the most notorious gangsters in Southwest Florida. We've also aided the Sanibel Police Department as well as the Cape Coral Sheriff's department to close the books on multiple murders, including the actor John Twist and two other individuals." Nugent allowed herself a satisfied smile. "Not a bad night's work. You should be pleased with yourself, Callister. We couldn't have cracked this case without your cooperation."

"Yeah, well, there's a problem," Tree said.

"What kind of problem would that be?" Nugent's satisfied expression remained resolutely in place.

"The problem is this: Carlos Chacal and Susan Tyler didn't kill anyone," Tree said. He had to force the words out of his bloodied mouth. "Correction, you are probably going to discover that Carlos killed his mistress's husband, Lenny, but he didn't kill Twist or those two other people."

Irritation had replaced Nugent's satisfaction. "Then who did?"

"I don't know. But it wasn't Chacal." Which was another lie.

He knew. Or thought he knew.

"And what makes you so sure?" The irritation was turning into anger.

"That's what Carlos and Susan told me before you blew them out of the water."

"They told you what you wanted to hear," pronounced Nugent.

"No what I really wanted to hear—what I *thought* was true—was that Susan Tyler as a young actress had been raped in Los Angeles by John Twist and now she was in Florida to get revenge with help from her lover, Carlos Chacal. But Susan wasn't raped by Twist. It was someone else. Twist had nothing to do with it. Susan and Carlos had no reason to kill Twist."

Nugent's rigidly set jaw was the telltale sign that Tree's declaration had not been well received. To put it mildly. She rose, looming over Tree, an FBI Valkyrie prepared to transport him into the depths of hell for daring to complicate her life. "Here's the thing, Callister," she said, jabbing a finger at him. "This case has been resolved. Perhaps not to everyone's satisfaction, but that almost never happens anyway. The perpetrators of the crimes have been dealt with. That is what counts. Do you understand that? Do I make myself clear?"

She waited for him to respond. When he didn't, just stared up at her with what he hoped was a look of defiance, she withdrew her finger and backed away in disgust. "Get him the hell out of my sight," she snapped at the other two agents.

"You want us to throw him overboard?" asked the balding agent. The idea didn't appear to bother him one way or the other. Another reason, Tree mused, why he didn't like water. Far too many people wanted to throw him into it.

"That's not a bad idea," said Nugent. She looked very serious when she said it. She made a gesture of resignation. "Maybe not. As soon as we dock, get him off the boat."

"You're making a mistake," Tree said.

Nugent glared at him. "By not throwing you overboard? You bet your ass I am."

Much to his surprise, they dropped Tree off at the Port Sanibel Marina adjacent to the Lighthouse Restaurant. Nugent gave him one last disgusted look. The balding agent said to him, "Better get your sorry ass under cover quick as you can."

"Why is that?"

"Reports coming in of a hurricane headed this way. A big one."

How appropriate, thought Tree. In addition to everything else tonight, now there was an oncoming hurricane. Life in Florida. The life of Tree Callister: teeth knocked out of his head one minute, almost shot the next, then nearly drowned, and now about to be swept away in a storm.

The wind had risen to the level of a shriek. It was all he could do to bend against it and get himself off the dock. The FBI boat in which Nugent and her fellow agents were traveling rolled violently in the choppy waters as it pulled away. It had begun to rain by the time he reached the cover of the Lighthouse Restaurant porch. His mouth was killing him. His body ached. He tried not to think about any of that as he entered the restaurant. He had to finish this. He had to confirm what he had been suspecting for a long time.

Roberto was just closing up for the night. The place was empty except for a few staff members cleaning up in the dining room. "You're a little late, Tree," Roberto said. "Surprised you're still around. Big storm coming."

"That's what I'm hearing," Tree said.

"If you don't my saying, you look like someone kicked you in the mouth."

"That's because someone did," Tree said. "Have you got a phone I could use?"

"Make it quick, will you? We're all trying to get out of here." Roberto produced his cellphone and handed it to Tree. "Just leave it on the bar when you're finished. Can I get you anything?"

"Just a glass of water, if you don't mind."

"Sure thing. You look like you could use it." Roberto went

behind the bar and ran a glass under a tap. He put the water on the bar. Tree nodded his thanks, took a deep gulp. The water settled some of the fire burning in his mouth. He took another drink and then put the glass aside so he could make the phone call he was dreading. He was hoping against hope that she wouldn't answer, that she was gone to a place where no one could find her. But she did answer, perhaps because she didn't realize it was him. Or maybe because she did.

"Gladys," he said. "It's me. Don't hang up."

"Why would I do that?" asked Gladys.

"It could be because you don't want to talk to me."

"I'll always talk to you, Tree. You do sound funny, though."

"That's because I've lost a couple of teeth," Tree said.

"I'm sorry to hear that," Gladys said. "You see what happens when I'm not there."

"I lose teeth," Tree said.

"What do you need, Tree?"

"A ride," Tree said.

"Okay."

"I'm at the Lighthouse," Tree said. "Why don't you pick me up outside?"

"I'm on my way," Gladys said.

34

Waiting on the porch outside, Tree watched in amazement as the palm trees in front of the restaurant nearly doubled over against the strengthening force of the wind. The rain came down in sheets now. Headlights flashed coming along Port Comfort Road. Gladys's truck turned into the parking lot. He went down the steps and dashed across to where she had parked. He fought with the wind to open the passenger door and climbed in.

Gladys gave him a quick glance, as he got the door closed. "You look like shit," she said.

"Thanks a lot." He leaned back in the seat, catching his breath. He felt gingerly at his mouth. "It's been a rough night."

"You'll have to tell me all about it," Gladys said, starting the truck forward. "But right now we should get you to a hospital."

"Let's go to the office first, okay? I've got to pick up a few things."

"Suit yourself," Gladys said quietly. "But you need to see a doctor."

As she brought the truck onto the roadway, a fierce wind gust whipped at the truck. Gladys gripped the wheel harder. Tree gave her a look as she picked up speed. "Aren't you worried about the hurricane?"

"I'm worried about a lot of things," Gladys said keeping her eyes fixed on the road. "A hurricane is the least of them."

She turned onto the Punta Rassa Road and then past the darkened Bimini Bait Shack and into the parking area outside the Cattle Dock Bait Company.

Gladys came to a stop and turned to Tree. "Now what?"

"Let's go inside."

"Yes, you have to pick up a few things," she said.

"That's right."

As they entered the darkened interior, the wind screamed through the open spaces, shaking the structure. They went into the Sunset Detective Agency Office. Tree flicked the switch but no lights came on. "It looks like we've lost power."

He turned to find Gladys standing expectantly in the dimness, her face stern, as though waiting for a fight. Tough Gladys, ready to take on all comers, Tree thought. Even him.

"Shell and Dix are dead," Tree said.

Gladys didn't react. She said, "Is that all you wanted to tell me?" Her voice was quiet, resigned.

"Not everything."

"I see," Gladys said. Her face betrayed nothing.

"Carlos Chacal. Ever heard of him?"

"No."

"He's a Florida drug lord. The FBI has been after him for years. They're very happy because he is dead too."

"I'm afraid my knowledge of Florida drug lords is limited," Gladys said noncommittally.

"His mistress was a woman named Susan Tyler. She used to be an actress in Hollywood."

"There were a lot of young actresses. They run in packs. I should know. I was in the pack."

"Susan was raped by a powerful figure while she was there. I thought the person who assaulted her was John Twist. Knowing that, it made sense that Susan, hearing that Twist was on Sanibel might come looking for revenge, helped by Carlos, a guy with a lot of experience when it comes to killing people."

"Sure," Glady said. "It makes sense."

"They made the mistake of thinking Twist had gone to the yacht to meet Shell Dean's fiancée. The assumption is that Carlos shot Bronco thinking he was Twist, then shot April because he's not the kind of guy who leaves witnesses. Later, he realized his mistake. Carlos then took out Twist at his house. The FBI likes that scenario. It's very convenient for them because they've been after Chacal for years. Now they don't have to go after him any longer. Case closed, as far as they're concerned."

"I imagine you played a major part in making the feds think the way they are thinking," Gladys said. The roar of the storm outside had become deafening. The building shook even more, as though determined to uproot itself.

"Yes, I'm afraid I did," Tree admitted. "Unfortunately, because of my assumptions, four people ended up getting killed tonight."

"You stumble into things that you shouldn't stumble into, Tree," Gladys said, speaking with authority. "You're out of your depth and people end up getting hurt. I guess maybe that's what happened tonight."

Tree nodded. "The deaths occurred out in the Gulf. An FBI operation. There are not going to be a lot of uncomfortable questions."

"Yes, that's very good," Gladys said. Her neutral expression hadn't altered, but she had relaxed somewhat, Tree noticed.

"However," he went on, "there is a problem with that scenario that the feds have so eagerly embraced."

"What sort of problem?" Gladys arranged an interested expression.

"None of it's true. I screwed up the whole thing. Not surprising, I suppose. Like you say, I stumble into things. I'm out of my depth. I get it wrong."

"What can I say, Tree?" Gladys said. "You do your best."

"Just after Carlos knocked out a couple of my teeth, Susan told me that, yes, she was raped in Hollywood, but not by John Twist. She and Carlos had no reason to murder Twist. Or Bronco Holiday and April May."

"If they're not the killers, then who?" Gladys had tensed again.

"It was right in front of me all the time," Tree said. "As usual, I either didn't believe or chose to believe something different." He fixed his eyes hard on Gladys. "I chose to believe you didn't go to the *Black Marlin*, mistake Bronco Holiday for Twist, shoot him, and then shoot April May. You were right there on the dock in front of me, but I wouldn't allow myself to believe it might have been you. And you played me so well, denying everything, and because I loved you, and you've protected me when I needed protection, I had to believe you—until, despite everything, I just can't do it any longer."

"I love you too, Tree," Gladys said. "You know that. You and Rex. Love you both."

"After you realized your mistake, you held off doing anything else—maybe having second thoughts—"

"I don't have second thoughts," Gladys interjected.

"But then Twist wanted to meet with you, atone for his sins, I suppose. You agreed to see him, went around to his house. I don't know whether you had anything planned, but when it turned out he hadn't changed, that he was the same monster who put you in the hospital years before…"

"If I repeated to you that he was alive when I left, would you believe me?"

"I would try hard, I suppose," Tree admitted. "Up to now, despite everything, I've forced myself into denial. I told myself over and over again that it wasn't you—couldn't have been you." Tree shook his head sadly. "But it was."

Gladys, silent, pensive, as though the accusation of murder required quiet consideration. Outside, the wind was like an oncoming freight train. Inside, it was if they were being shaken around in a shoe box. From the bait area came the sound of shattering glass.

Gladys had to raise her voice to be heard over the din. "We'd better get out of here. This is really getting bad."

"I haven't said anything to the police," Tree said. "I'm assuming that when they get the ballistic results back from the murders and realize the same gun was used, questions will be asked, and it won't be long until they trace it back to your gun."

"You mean the SIG Sauer." With Gladys you never quite knew where the gun came from, but there was no doubting it now was in her hand.

"Yeah, that's the one," Tree said.

"I do love you, Tree." Was that a catch in Gladys's otherwise firm monotone? Tree couldn't be sure. "I loved Rex too in my own crazy way. I loved working in an office where I was supposed to answer the phone. Only the phone never rang and I ended up spending most of my time getting you out of the various messes you got yourself into."

"You saved my ass many times."

"But here's the thing, Tree. Here's a mess neither one of us can get out of easily. Maybe not at all."

"No," said Tree.

His voice was lost in the high screech of the wind that also drowned out Gladys's response as she raised the gun. At the same time, the roof above them seemed to burst as the force of the wind ripped at it, sending parts of it flying into the night. Rain poured down in torrents. A loud cracking caused Tree to look up in time to see one of the ceiling beams crash down, just missing him but sending him sprawling back onto the floor.

Pieces of the thatched roof descended as Tree crawled under his desk. More roof fragments came down. The wind whistled even louder as rain poured through the open roof.

Tree rose to his feet, clambered over the beam, fearing that Gladys had been hit full on. He called her name, frantically digging through plaster and wood. He couldn't see her. He was soaking wet as he made his way out through the bait shop.

Surging water from San Carlos Bay swirled above his ankles as he staggered outside. The force of the wind nearly knocked him over. Tree could see the roof tearing off the nearby Bimini Bait Shack. Peering through the opaque mist of the hard-falling rain, wreckage soaring past, Tree searched for Gladys's pickup truck.

It was gone.

Behind him, the Cattle Dock Bait Company began to come apart. Tree could hardly believe what he was seeing. He ducked a piece of siding and staggered blindly up a narrow embankment, trying to get away from the devastation unfolding behind him. He reached Punta Rassa Road. To his right, a section of the bridge to Sanibel collapsed into the heaving waters of San Carlos Bay.

"Tree! Tree!" a voice called.

He turned to see an SUV coming to a stop along the road. Freddie leaned out the window, her face filling with relieved anguish. "Get in!" she yelled.

His angel. His savior arrived in the nick of time to save him.

What would he ever do without her, his shelter from the storm?

35

Searchlights splashed the towering pagoda of Grauman's Chinese Theatre, the newest and most dramatic of the many movie palaces lining Hollywood Boulevard. The huge crowd outside the theatre was more like an unruly mob delirious with excitement in its appreciation as the greatest stars of the cinema arrived in big, shiny cars for the worldwide premiere of *The King of Kings*.

Tree found himself on the red carpet leading to the theatre's forecourt, jostled by arriving celebrities in their movie premiere finery, eagerly chatting away as they pushed past. Several arrivals glanced at him and did a double take. What's the matter? Tree wondered. Why were these glamorous people staring at him? He looked down at himself and saw to his horror that he was naked except for the loincloth he had worn on the cross. He was at the premiere of *The King of Kings* in a loincloth. Little wonder he was getting shocked stares.

"There you are my young, dubious Jesuit friend," said Cecil B. DeMille. "Glad you're here." He wore a black tie and tux, tanned and flushed, his eyes agleam. "I just want you to know we never used the stuff we shot with you. That drunken fool Warner sobered up long enough so that we could get the scenes we needed."

"But I'm standing here wearing a loincloth, Mr. DeMille," Tree said in a panicked voice. "How did that happen?"

DeMille seemed not to notice Tree's panic. "Look around

you, young man," he enthused. "Take in the excitement these people are experiencing. They are made ecstatic with joy, generated by the movies—the most powerful medium on earth!"

"But what am I doing in a loincloth?" Tree demanded.

"And this is only the beginning," went on DeMille, ignoring Tree's plight. "The motion picture will go to places we cannot imagine, accomplish things that are beyond our capacity to grasp. Their future is limitless!"

"Movies will talk, I can tell you that much is certain," Tree asserted.

DeMille gave him a sharp, horrified look. "Are you out of your mind, young man? Do not buy into this momentary distraction of so-called 'talkies.' The beauty of motion pictures lies in their visual power. That power is enhanced by their silence. To break that silence is to give up the dreamlike quality inherent in the very presence of the motion picture image. To sit in a movie palace full of like-minded strangers, you are not seeing a movie—you are in a dream!"

"I hate tell you this, Mr. DeMille, but you're so wrong," Tree said as the two of them were jostled by incoming guests. "Pretty soon synchronized sound will change movies forever. They will never be the same again. The whole way of life you are part of tonight will all disappear. You think this is the beginning but in fact it's the end. It will be as though all this never existed."

DeMille reacted furiously. "You ill-informed fool! How dare you stand there half-naked to tell me, the man who founded Hollywood, who practically single-handedly created movies, and you dare to tell me that all this is finished."

He frantically motioned to nearby police officers struggling to restrain the surging crowd. "Get this madman out of here," he shouted to the officers. "He's an uninvited interloper—and

he's not wearing any clothes! Get him out of my sight. Now!"
Immediately, Tree was set upon by two police officers who
grabbed him roughly as onlookers began to curse. In the background, he could hear DeMille yelling, "He is a blasphemer! A
blasphemer, I tell you!"

"He hates movies!" someone screamed. The next thing,
people were hitting at him as they swarmed around, wrench-
ing him away from the police, throwing him to the ground.
It was like something out of the riot in *The Day of the Locust.*
Here were the locusts, coming at him for the crime of destroying their dreams, kicking at him mercilessly, bellowing that he
must die for the monstrous crime of hating movies—*hating*
them!

Tree screamed and screamed and screamed....

"Tree! For God's sake!" Freddie looked genuinely alarmed
as her husband jerked awake.

"Where am I?" he demanded in a daze.

"You're in a hotel room in Los Angeles." Freddie was shaking her head. "What's wrong with you anyway?"

"I was nearly naked in front of Grauman's Chinese Theatre.
Cecil B. DeMille screamed at me and then turned the crowd
outside the theatre on me because they said I hated movies."

"Well, you don't hate movies," Freddie asserted. "Get up
and get dressed. You are going to the premiere of the... *movie*
of your best friend's life."

Well, maybe not quite a movie, Tree thought. Not a movie
Cecil. B. DeMille would recognize, but close enough, considering the times he was living in. Tree would not be wearing a
loincloth, thankfully. It was all just a dream. He was lost in his
dreams.

The crowd gathered outside what was now TLC Chinese Theatre, one of the few surviving relics from Hollywood's fleeting golden age of silence, was not nearly as thick as the one in his dream.

Klieg lights did not light up the evening to blast the front of the towering pagoda that, astonishingly, had loomed over the history of movies ever since DeMille introduced *The King of Kings* at the theatre. But uniformed police were still present to restrain what crowd there was. A sleek publicist guided arrivals along the red carpet, replete with tux-clad security men, seemingly chosen because of their resemblance to refrigerators.

Tree and Freddie helped Rex Baxter out of the limousine. He wore dark glasses and a tuxedo. Freddie looked smashing in a Ralph Lauren gown. Tree, matching Rex, also had rented a traditional tuxedo for the occasion. They were back in Hollywood. This was Rex's big night, even though he had not ended up playing himself.

"I'm nervous as a cat," said Rex as they moved forward to pose in front of a big poster advertising the Netflix series. It featured Harrison Ford who, Tree had to concede, made a pretty good Rex. He had yet to arrive, thus the platoon of photographers had to satisfy themselves with Rex and his two friends. To the photographers' credit, they actually seemed enthusiastic and even made sure Rex removed his sunglasses.

A young publicist in a black cocktail dress, smiling eagerly, approached. "I'm going to take our star away," she said. "There are reporters dying to talk to you, Mr. Baxter."

"I'd prefer to stick with these two," Rex said.

Freddie took his hand and gave him a loving look. "Off you go, darling Rex. This is your night. Talk to everyone. Enjoy it."

He gave Freddie a kiss and then a hug for Tree. "I love you both," he said.

"Love you right back," Tree said.

It was hard to tell, but Tree was pretty sure he saw a tear in Rex's eye.

Freddie and Tree moved to one side. "Let's go in," Freddie said to him. Once again, he couldn't help think how his wife still managed to take his breath away, so elegant tonight, ageless in Ralph Lauren, her blond hair lustrous. He drew her to him. "Just want to savor the moment," Tree said.

"No bad dreams," Freddie murmured, taking his hand.

"Not tonight, anyway. We've got a lot to deal with when we get back."

"The house can be repaired, thank goodness," Freddie said. "We got off luckier than so many other people."

"We did," Tree agreed. He held her closer, thinking of what could have happened, and didn't—thanks to Freddie's timely rescue.

Not far away, Tree could hear Rex as he was interviewed by a female reporter holding a microphone that said she was from the *Entertainment Tonight* TV show. The woman had long black hair that fell to her waist. She looked more like a star than the stars she was interviewing, Tree thought.

"Mr. Baxter, Harrison is getting raves for his performance as you," the reporter stated. "How do you feel about that?"

"I've always said that only Indiana Jones could play me," Rex answered. "It looks like I was right."

"But it's a role Harrison almost didn't play," the reporter continued. "Originally, John Twist, the legendary 1950s movie star, came out of retirement to portray you in the series."

"That's right," Rex said guardedly.

"But John Twist was murdered shortly before he completed filming, and I understand that initially there was some consideration of you taking over. Is that true?"

"Yes, but the character is so complex, so unique, that I felt it needed one of the best actors in the business," Rex said. "Thankfully, we got him. Harrison did a great job, like everyone is saying. From here on in, I'm going to act more like Harrison Ford."

"So is it fair to say that it all worked out better than you could ever have imagined?" the reporter asked with a smile.

"Not better than I imagined," Rex retorted. "But pretty darned good."

Tree glanced around taking in the crowd. He drew to a stop to focus on a woman barely visible in the twilight. She looked a lot like Gladys Demchuk, the former Blue Streak. Her gaze seemed riveted on Rex.

Rex finished the interview, turned and spotted the woman among the onlookers. The two looked at each other. Rex smiled and nodded.

No, Tree thought, it couldn't be. It was not possible that Gladys murdered John Twist in part so that Rex—

No, he wouldn't allow his mind to go there. It was impossible. It didn't work in the end, if that was the plan. But still…

"What is it?" Freddie asked, seeing the expression on his face.

He looked again into the crowd. Gladys had vanished. Rex was on his way into the theatre. He was seeing things, he decided. He had been seeing a lot of things lately that weren't there.

"I must have been mistaken," he said. "I thought I saw something that I didn't really see."

"You do a lot of that," she said.

"I love you more than anything in the world." His voice choked a bit as he finished.

"Are you sure you're, okay?" Freddie clasped his hand even more firmly. "I'm worried about you—more than ever lately. It's been a crazy time."

"It has, but as long as I have you, I'm fine," he said.

"You have me," Freddie confirmed. "At least until the end of the century. Then I'll review the situation and decide where we go from there."

"This is reassuring news," Tree said.

"I thought it might be," she replied.

Still holding his hand, Freddie led him inside the theatre. As they came into the lobby, Tree spotted an imposing bald man, very tanned, incongruously wearing jodhpurs. When he spotted Tree, the tanned man mouthed something.

Unless Tree missed his guess, the tanned man said, "I told you so."

Acknowledgements

For thirteen years each November, I would drive over the causeway leading to Sanibel Island, pristine in the bright sunshine illuminating the calm waters of San Carlos Bay, on my way to introduce a new Sanibel Sunset Detective novel into the small world I inhabited.

I spent most days working up and down the island, at Bailey's General Store, at MacIntosh Books, Gene's Books, Adventures in Paradise, Jerry's Foods, and then on to Captiva Island for the Bubble Room Emporium. To quote Arthur Miller, I was "a man out there in the blue, riding on a smile and a shoeshine."

If I wasn't on Sanibel or Captiva, I would drive over to Fort Myers Beach, spending Saturday nights on the street in front of Pete's Bar dazzled by the honkytonk excitement of the pedestrian area that had been dubbed Times Square, a band playing at the end of the street, kids with absolutely no interest fleeing past a guy with a grin on his face and a book in his hand.

Each week I would drive out Estero Boulevard to the far reaches of Fort Myers Beach where Annette's Book Nook was located. The wonderful Annette Stillson was always welcoming and there were fewer kids and a lot more readers.

I got to know everyone, residents and visitors, many of whom became loyal Sanibel Sunset Detective readers. I formed friendships, heard often amazing stories of love and loss, embracing readers broken by some unfolding tragedy in their lives, accompanied by much laughter with the delightful and intelligent women who make up the majority of my readership.

I had to steel myself beforehand, but once I got out there doing the book signings and promotions, speaking to book clubs, I thoroughly enjoyed myself, the warmth of people and the sunshine. This was my annual routine. It would go on forever.

Then, out of nowhere, it was all gone. Overnight an island and its way of life was wiped out. The causeway I loved to drive over became impassable. Sanibel was cut off. The lively madness of Times Square had been reduced to rubble. Lives were upended and ruined. The people whose generosity I had relied on for so many years were out of business. How the islands, Fort Myers Beach, and the surrounding city of Fort Myers, ever come back from this devastation is hard to imagine. It is happening as I write this, but it is happening slowly.

Sanibel Island—with lots of help from my brother, Ric—changed the life of a writer who feared he was finished professionally. Thanks to the island and its people I found my footing again. I had no idea how much all of this meant to me until it ended so abruptly.

Sadly, heartbreakingly, my life has been forever changed once again. I wrestled with that reality returning to Southwest Florida months after Hurricane Ian had struck, shocked by the devastation not only on Sanibel but particularly on Fort Myers Beach, which has been rightly described as looking like a war zone.

How to handle such a catastrophic reality in what are supposed to be light-hearted mystery novels? How do you use a setting that if it has not changed forever, will certainly be much different for years to come and will probably never return to the way it was?

I'm not sure I've done the right thing—whether there even is a right thing—but I opted for the Sanibel that exists in the pages of fourteen Tree Callister novels, the island where nothing ever happens—except something always happens to Tree Callister. A hurricane would play a part at the end, but maybe not the hurricane that was Ian. Perhaps a hurricane that would exist in the world of these novels.

As I came to the end of this book, sitting in Fort Myers, I couldn't help but think about all the people who over the years have made the Sanibel Sunset Detective possible. I have to give another big shoutout to my brother Ric who in addition to prodding me to write something set in Southwest Florida, has overseen production of the books' interiors with patience and professionalism.

My wife, Kathy, not only provided so much love and support, but also has tirelessly acted as first reader. Ray Bennett and David Kendall diligently saved me from myself many, many times, as did Alexandra Lenhoff, aka my sister-in-law. Susie Holly on Sanibel Island also edited a number of the later books.

Lately, the eagle-eyed James Bryan Simpson has become an unexpected treasure illuminating the author's many shortcomings in order to make his work so much better than it ever would have been otherwise. He has done extraordinary work on *The Sanibel Sunset Detective Goes to the Movies*.

Finally, a deep bow to Jennifer Smith who has produced small miracles of design for most of the covers.

Many, many thanks to all of you. I can't tell you how much your help has meant to me. I am forever grateful.

As I finish writing *The Sanibel Sunset Detective Goes to the Movies*, I grapple with one final question: Will Tree return?

We will see…

COMING SOON

THE

SANIBEL

SUNSET

DETECTIVE'S

LAST CASE

Is this the end of Tree?

MISS PRISCILLA TEMPEST

KINDLY REQUESTS YOUR ATTENTION...

DEATH AT THE SAVOY

"Entertaining series launch... This light, frothy mystery is perfect escapist fare."

Publisher's Weekly

A dead body at the Savoy? Impossible! Suspected of murder, her job on the line, Priscilla had better get to the bottom of what happened in suite 705—and do it fast.

A plucky heroine! The world's most famous hotel! Swinging 1960s London in full swing! Lots of champagne! A bit of humor! And—death at the Savoy!

SCANDAL AT THE SAVOY

"The return of the glamorous Priscilla Tempest in *Scandal at the Savoy* is an occasion for great celebration."

Michael Rowe, Shirley Jackson Award-finalist author of Wild Fell and Enter, Night

The fabulously rich and famous, are converging on the iconic Savoy Hotel in swinging '60s London—a famous Broadway producer with anger issues, a demanding rajah from India, a gorgeous British film star with certain kinky predilections. In short, all is as it should be—until the mysterious death of a notorious showgirl threatens to scandalize the hotel.

AVAILABLE AT AMAZON.COM